OF

LIGHTNING

AND

TOPAZ

THE WEATHER COURT GEM SERIES

KC SILVER

To those who shine their lights when others are lost in the dark.

One

S tained glass windows haunted her dreams. Her dreams haunted her.

A golden glow seeped through a mosaic of shattered glass. As the morning sun began to rise, its rays directed a twinkling spotlight at the altar. The shine was blinding, the bright weather a rarity in the Lightning Court—an appreciated reprieve from the usual gloomy, gray skies.

Piora fiddled with her hands in her lap, pulling the sleeves of her knit sweater up past her wrists, her head downcast into the high neck of the gray wool.

Soon the service would begin. As others slid into the pews, awaiting the peaceful music and profound words of the minister, Piora's mind was spinning. This time could be spent ideating her Undertaking invention, but she knew the importance of praying to the Weather Gods—especially Elektra, the Goddess of Lightning. They would bless her with the perfect use of her powers and skills.

Someone nudged Piora as they squeezed by her to take a seat. The chapel was busier than usual. She had no clue why. It wasn't a holiday nor was it near the Undertaking quite yet; they still had a few months until then. At that time, the entire court congregated together and prayed intensely for another successful Undertaking so that the powers of the court could be replenished. It was the one time of year when the court felt unified, instead of the divide everyone fabricated.

This year, some of the responsibility fell on Piora. She was part of the cohort of four other participants. At only twenty-three, she was surprised to have been picked already. She anticipated having to enter her name until the maximum age of participation. Yet, the Gods blessed her with the opportunity to prove herself now. She would *not* take it for granted.

Before she could dwell on her nerves too long, a chord from the piano sounded, and her mother walked in with ivory and gold robes swishing behind her. Her long, blonde hair swayed past her hips, framing her light face and rosy cheeks. Since being designated the court minister ten years ago, she hadn't cut her hair. Following her mother's lead, Piora hadn't cut her brassy hair—a smidge darker than her mother's—either, but she preferred to keep it tightly braided and wound to the back of her head. It was a nuisance otherwise.

As the music swelled, the congregation stood, and Piora got a better look at whose deft fingers played.

Piora now understood why the crowd was larger.

The man had his eyes closed, but even then he was captivating. His brown hair was closely shaved to his head. On others it would look unusual and wrong, but on him, it made sense for some reason, like it was done for a purpose other than looks. His fingers moved across the keys with swift ease, the rings on his fingers gleaming in the light. He looked at peace, and like he belonged—like a king on his throne, holding court.

Piora had been so distracted by the magnificence of his hands that when she lifted her gaze to his face, she almost gasped upon finding his golden brown eyes, edging on the side of yellow, staring right at her. They practically glowed—like two topaz gemstones, the same gemstone of the Heart of this court. For some reason, a deep ache radiated in Piora's chest, not of pain, but a storm of emotions. The music had never called to her like this before, and yet the power the notes held almost made her knees buckle. Everyone else seemed unaffected, but she was in a trance, her body rendered powerless by his enchanting tune.

Then, like a bucket of cold water splashing over flushed skin, the music came to an abrupt halt as her mother's words boomed from the voice-elevation device.

A shudder wracked through Piora's body.

"A blessed day to all," her mother started, her tone even and confident. "As always, we thank the holy Weather Gods for the gifts they bestow on us. We thank Elektra for the lightning that pumps through the veins of the gifted."

Piora had despised the word "gifted," ever since she was a child. It was a way to separate those with powers—like her—from those who didn't. Not everyone in the court had the ability to wield lightning. Hence, the divide between the "gifted" and the giftless. Her mother, though not bestowed with such gifts, was awarded the gift of Sight. That was why she had been named the minister of the court. It was a rare power. One not taken lightly.

Piora was born with the power to do both, though she would never admit it out loud that she had dreams from the Gods, ones she knew—should she accept her calling—would turn prophetic. She had no idea if anyone else in the Lightning Court also struggled with dreams, but Piora assumed once she won the Undertaking and declined the Gods' call for her to become minister, someone else would step up. Only her mother knew the truth of her powers, because when she was a child, Piora once sought her mother's comfort after having a nightmare. Piora had explained the dream, and her mother had shot up from the bed in delight. She had explained to Piora that the dreams were good tidings: that she was destined to become the future minister with this newfound power.

But Piora always felt more in tune with her lightning powers, and preferred to utilize those instead. Her mother was displeased by her daughter's decision. Now Piora had something to prove; she would win this year's Undertaking, win the honor of the Gods choosing her invention, and be bestowed the Heart—all if only to spite her mother, and her desperate desire to have her daughter follow in her footsteps.

"I'd also like to thank, Izyk, for joining us today, and blessing us with his musical presence. His ability to move a room is exactly how the Gods intended us to celebrate them."

The pianist—Izyk, Piora supposed—bit his lip, as if he were trying to hold back a laugh; his golden eyes alight with arrogance, like he didn't need the praise.

"We now begin with a prayer."

Piora had attended these gatherings too many times, and the services were all the same. The same prayers, the same songs, the same words of "wisdom" from her mother.

May the Gods guide us towards a prosperous path and bless us with power to choose correctly.

She refrained from rolling her eyes when the words struck exactly towards Piora and her predicament. Instead, Piora allowed her mind to wander as her mother droned. Her eyes wandered, too—back to the piano.

Izyk's hands grasped the wooden bench as his eyes began to gloss over. He obviously didn't want to be here, either. So, why was he? He wouldn't be receiving any coin from this work.

The congregation finally took their seats, and Piora followed, the whole affair now muscle memory. The creeks of the old wooden pews were swallowed by the sounds of the piano beginning again.

Piora watched closely, and the pianist's movements were so precise that it appeared like his fingers floated across the piano. She wondered if she would see him again after this service, or if he realized his mistake in volunteering, and would avoid returning.

One moment he was out in the streets with his violin, and the next, he was being asked if he wanted an opportunity for some exposure.

Izyk, as an opportunist, of course said yes. Plus, perhaps an hour spent praising the pointless Gods would inspire him. His recent compositions had been stale, lackluster. Nothing worthy of being played for an audience.

He needed a muse. Something that would take his music to new heights. Ludwik, his closest and only friend, said he needed to slow down and get a venue first. Izyk always shrugged off his friend's sensible suggestions. Everything would work out in time.

He didn't listen to minister Kaplana's words, though—he found them dreadful and dull. How many times could someone thank the Gods in such a short period? Surely, the Gods themselves would be bored of it, too.

When he ended the last song of the service with a flair of his wrists, the congregation stood and quietly walked out . He remained seated at the piano; he wanted the silence, at least for a little. It was so rare for him to get it these days. Living on top of a tavern meant struggling to drown out the noise of patrons as he tried to sleep.

Instead of being met with silence, he heard someone clear their throat. He could guess who it belonged to. A mysterious woman from the farthest pew in the back had been staring at him, and he had clocked it. He didn't mind the attention though.

"I don't think it was smart that you played so well. My mother is going to bind you to the piano so you must play again," the woman said. He had noticed her throughout the whole service;

something about her didn't fit in with the rest of the crowd. While the congregation was earnestly reverent, she seemed like she was acting a part in a play. She stepped closer to him, and right as she hit a beam of sunlight, her dark eyes sparkled. There were threads of gold weaved throughout the stormy blues. It was a sign that she was gifted. All those with lightning powers had the golden marks. He wouldn't be surprised that under her modest clothes, she hid more of the beautiful gold he was envious of. His marks were an eyesore by comparison.

He cocked his head to the right. "Minister Kaplana is your mother?"

She huffed. "Unfortunately."

"She's very devout."

The woman shrugged. "It's part of the job."

"And are you her protégé?" he asked with a smile on his face, only teasing to rile her up. There was no way she also had the Sight if lightning coursed through her veins.

She ignored his question. "I just wanted to tell you that you played beautifully...I didn't catch your name."

If Izyk saw it clearly, then there was a blush staining her ivory cheeks. It was a common response to his presence, but he liked the look of it on her more than the others for some reason.

"It's Izyk," he offered. "And it's easy to play a song already written."

"I doubt that. Your skill is like magic, Izyk."

He internally winced. "Well, some of us had to make due, since the Gods refused to gift us with *actual* magic."

Her eyes widened while she bit her bottom lip, as if shutting herself up before she could say anything more. He wanted to pull it out from under her teeth, he wanted to hear her voice; something about the mixture of her seriousness, her curtness, and her genuine kindness captivated him.

Instead, she whirled around, gathered her belongings from the pew, and left.

Sparks flew by her as she headed to her station. The workshop was already crowded, and she was the last one to arrive. She nodded a quick greeting to Professor Silo, who acknowledged her tardiness by pointing to the clock. Piora mouthed an *I'm sorry*. He waved her off, not actually reprimanding her, for he understood where she had been this morning.

"Hope your mother didn't bore you too much," Daria said.

Piora put a smile on her face and increased her pitch to a friendly tone as she faced her friend.

"Not at all," Piora waved away the notion of that possibility. "I love starting my days with prayers to the Gods."

Daria brushed her dark, coiled braids over her shoulder. "Even if it means you start late?"

"I work better under pressure."

Daria hummed. "Is that how you almost caused an explosion last week when Professor Silo said that we only had an hour remaining before the doors would be locked for the night?"

"*That* was because Roksana started pulling my hair. It's not my fault she left her stuff in the middle of a walking space, and I stepped on it."

"Excuses," her friend muttered under her breath as she started to tinker with a prototype in front of her on the workstation.

Piora stared at the inventions enviously before turning her attention down to her own sketches. She flipped through her ideas, but none of them spoke to her; none of them felt like *the one*.

They had a few months until the Undertaking, but it would take time to build the actual item, test it, and clean it up to be usable. This was not a time where she could fail. Too many eyes were on her, and she was the one who had pushed for this opportunity.

She needed the Heart to pick her invention as the winner. Only then could she finally prove to her mother that she was more than her protégé, as Izyk had put it.

She was just waiting for that spark to hit her.

Two

Izyk finished the last chord on his violin. A small crowd had circled him, but once the music ended, only a handful tossed a coin in the metal cup by his feet.

The market bustled around him, a populous area prime for busking, yet he left each day with just enough to scrounge for a loaf of bread and some dried meat.

Everyone cared more for the newest invention that was being sold than his pitiful tunes. Last year's Undertaking winner was a portable heating device, allowing the market to now sell hot soups and teas fresh to its patrons. To be fair, he could at least appreciate that one, because it meant the market sellers made more money at the end of the day.

Still, he despised the direction the Lightning Court was moving. The changes that wouldn't stop. Sooner or later, musicians would no longer be needed, and art would no longer be craved. *He* would become a ghost, easily forgotten, just like the abandoned streets of this town, where so many of the giftless had been pushed out into the outskirts of the court.

He had been lucky that he had been able to travel to other courts during his early days, most predominantly the Sun Court that ran alongside the Lightning Court's border. The Royal family in the Sun Court enjoyed the traditional music he played for their vivacious parties, and he had a reprieve from the gray skies of the Lightning Court while being surrounded by greenery and light. Those opportunities had dwindled over the years. Plus, he wanted to settle down at some point, and expand his music to a full orchestra. He just needed a place to make those dreams a reality.

He went up to a stall selling bread stuffed with cheese and he splurged on it, if only to cheer his mood. His hands were cold, the bright sun deceiving. Still, he appreciated the shine. He knew it would be temporary.

"Your music lulled my child to sleep," the vendor moved aside to reveal a small babe wrapped up in fur blankets as it laid on a cot, oblivious to the bustle around them.

"Am I that boring?" he teased.

The woman smiled back at him, but shook her head. "Peaceful. A nice break from the usual chaos."

"Well I'm glad to be of service." Izyk bowed his head.

In a show of gratitude, she gave him the roll for free, even after he insisted on paying. Apparently the child had been crying for days because he had been teething. Izyk had done her a favor.

Right as he turned to go, a weight landed on his shoulder.

He turned his attention to his flying friend, whose navy blue feathers began shifting Izyk's coat to the same color. A magical bird—the size of his forearm—that no one knew where it came from, as evidenced by the slow wave of eyes widening at the display of its abilities. The bird was one-of-a-kind, to Izyk's knowledge.

"Show off," Izyk muttered to Potek, as he heard some *oohs* and *ahs* from unwanted gawkers. Where were these people when he had been playing? Izyk considered bringing the bird into his act, but if he didn't have food to incentivize him, Potek would start pecking at him, no doubt.

"You seem to have an extra sense that tells you exactly when I have food in my hands, don't you, Potek?"

The bird adjusted its feet to steady itself as it croaked. A resounding yes, then.

Sighing, Izyk ripped off a small, cheese-less piece of bread, and fed it to the wild animal. Potek had been around for as long as Izyk could remember. Everyday, Izyk was surprised when he didn't find the bird dead in a ditch. Perhaps the Gods took mercy on Izyk; they saw he needed an extra companion since he had no family, and only one other friend. However, this wasn't a symbiotic relationship. Potek took advantage of Izyk's kindness—but that didn't stop Izyk from helping the poor thing.

Izyk weaved through various stalls, peeking at the different wares being sold—from the jewelry, to the clothes, to the shoes—all of it uniquely handmade. Nothing he could afford, but pretty, nonetheless. Potek tried swiping at some of the items, and when Potek got too feisty, Izyk shooed him to fly away to only the Gods knew where.

There were a few carts with Undertaking inventions, where everything looked the same. The same mechanisms that did the same thing. He didn't dawdle too long at those shops, refusing to give them attention that they didn't deserve. The same couldn't be said for the rest of the villagers, as they all practically climbed over themselves for a look.

Izyk rolled his eyes at the clamor, pushing through. He made it into a clear area right as someone tried to break into the crowd. They bumped shoulders, and he could hear the woman swear under her breath as her bag toppled, and a cloud of papers dispersed over the ground.

In a frenzy, the woman bent down and tried to collect the papers, blocking everyone's path.

Izyk watched his feet, careful to not step on any of the woman's papers, but the crowd was not as gracious as him. Shoes trampled through the pile, and the woman squeaked in horror, the sound harsh to his ears.

He kicked a person's calf lightly, and swiped a paper free as the stranger stumbled onwards.

"Apologies," Izyk said as he outstretched his hand with the paper. "Looks like you dropped this." The woman picked up the last paper before she finally lifted her head to him. Izyk held in his gasp.

It was her. The woman at yesterday's service, the one with the dark eyes. In this afternoon light, the golden veins glowed, showing how they held the power of lightning within them. Her hair, like yesterday, was tightly bound on her head.

"You pushed me," she muttered so quietly that he barely heard her.

He crossed his arms. "You clearly weren't paying attention to the crowd. Didn't anyone tell you to watch where you're going?"

She blinked up at him, perhaps finally recognizing him.

"You're right," she said, readjusting her tone. "I wasn't paying attention to where I was going."

She didn't offer any further explanation as she was swallowed by the crowd. Izyk stood there, stunned for a moment, before someone pushed him.

"Don't block the way!" The passerby yelled.

Izyk shrugged off the encounter with the woman before he kept on his way again.

The cobbled streets were quieter, but it would soon pick up once everyone was racing to get back home for the night.

Birds squawked from their perches on homes and trees, investigating the ground for any food. Potek was nowhere in sight. Izyk broke a small piece of bread and threw it behind him. He could feel the breeze as the birds dived for it.

Entering his home, Ludwik greeted him from behind the bar. His friend was drying glasses. There were a few patrons already inside the bar, sipping on amber colored ale. Izyk's mouth watered. He could use a drink.

He sat down at the bar, and without needing to be asked, Ludwik poured him a glass.

"No luck, again?"

Izyk pulled a pouch from his pocket, one that was too light for his liking. Ludwik's lips tightened at the sight.

"Maybe once we're closer to the Undertaking, it will pick up. Everyone is more generous when their lives are at stake," his friend reassured him.

Izyk laughed dryly. "You think everyone will be scared the Gods will damn them if they don't help fund my dreams?"

"It will happen, Izyk."

"We'll see." Izyk sighed, then gulped down his drink. Dribbles ran down his chin and neck, but he didn't bother wiping them away, just headed upstairs to his room. Ludwik had been kind enough to let Izyk stay here, only paying a small rent so that he could save enough money to buy the old, abandoned music hall. He had been trying for years, and he was still far from the asking price.

He reached into his inside chest pocket and looked at the pocket watch. He didn't need the time—he kept the blasted thing next to his heart as a reminder of how time wasn't stopping. If he didn't get enough money soon, all his work would be for nothing.

"There you are," Piora's mother said from the kitchen. "I need your help."

Piora hoped to have sneaked past her mother. She'd had a long day at the workshop, and her mind felt like it was put through a meat grinder. Everyone in this year's cohort had either decided on their invention or narrowed it down to two. Piora was the only one left who hadn't.

She stepped into the kitchen, where a kettle was on the stove and a pot of soup was boiling. The smell of onion wafted in the air.

Her mother waved her over, where Piora was greeted with an array of flowers on the kitchen table. "I have a burial tomorrow, and I need to put together bouquets for the grave."

Piora's shoulders sank, but she sat down, grabbed some roses, and started arranging them. A little after her mother first took on the role of minister, she decided on creating this new tradition for herself. Apparently, at her first burial, the grave was empty because the deceased had no living family or friends. Her mother had been so haunted by the bleakness of it that she would never allow that to happen again.

Piora stuck a flower into the glass vase, one intricately designed by those gifted with powers. The lightning in one's veins could be destructive, but some had a special control, like the lightning was an extension of their fingertips; these gifted few were able to draw fine details with it. Piora's magic—along with her other fellow inventors—lay somewhere in the middle.

"Any progress?" her mother asked without giving her daughter a glance. Her long hair was behind her ears to keep it from getting in her face, but even when she was busily working, she refused to put it up.

"Not yet." Piora hesitated but then decided to confide in her mother. "I want to create something that will be so useful, that people will wonder how they ever existed without it. It needs to be something great, because that's the only way the Heart and Gods will think it worthy."

Her mother took a deep breath. "Usefulness is subjective."

Piora did not think that was true at all. Usefulness meant it needed to serve a purpose that would make everything better. No one would use things that just wasted space.

"I keep waiting for something to hit me, for when it all makes sense."

"I think you can't push things to always work. Sometimes you just need to follow what is meant for you."

Not this again. Piora rolled her eyes as she kept her attention on the flowers. Her mother desperately wanted her to follow her in her steps as minister, and she believed that Piora would answer the call soon. Too bad that the Gods had been knocking for years, and Piora refused to let them in.

"Or maybe," Piora countered, "sometimes the Gods are trying to test us to see how willing we are to work for the futures we are destined for."

"The Gods aren't there to confuse us, darling. They are there to guide us."

"Well, I feel guided towards winning the Undertaking by having the *best* invention."

Her mother gave her a flat look, as if she was chastising a child for being difficult. All conversations surrounding the Undertaking ended this way with her mother. Her mother called her stubborn, but Piora considered herself determined. If only determination was enough to spark a winning idea.

Piora put the finishing touches on her bouquet, and stormed off upstairs to her room. She couldn't have a civil discussion with her mother about this; it would only turn into arguing, and that time could be better spent on finding the perfect invention.

She had been running from her dreams from the Gods for too long to let her mother force her into becoming a minister. She couldn't do that, and never would. As soon as she woke up from that first dream where the Gods had tied her down and told her that her life would forever be committed to them, she decided she would build another path for herself. The day her lightning powers manifested, she sobbed in relief with the knowledge that greater possibilities opened up for her.

Three

A brisk wind seeped into Izyk's bones. He wrapped his old wool coat tighter around his body. He had been up early, walking the waterfront path, where it was quiet in the morning. Since he spent most of his days practicing or performing music, he needed those moments of peace before starting the day. Without it, the constant noise would become too much. Plus, he always felt a burst of inspiration after watching the crashing sea, and feeling the salt air on his skin.

Now, as he headed back to town, the sun hid behind a wall of clouds.

He would spend his day busking in the market again. Some days he felt like he was setting himself up for failure. He did the same thing almost everyday with hopes of a better outcome, but it never came. That's why he had taken the job performing at the service. He had wanted to expose himself to a different crowd, thinking that someone would notice him, and offer him a higher paying job. Unfortunately, no one had come up to him. Only that beautiful woman who complimented him; but as much as he appreciated her attention, her adoration hadn't won him the coin he needed.

He tapped a pencil against his hand as he walked, listening to the sounds around him. A rhythmic beat formed in his head, and he homed in on it. He pushed his mind to keep it going, to find the heart of the sound. It had been months since something new had sparked, and he didn't want to lose it.

He picked up the pace, now drumming the pencil against the gray brick building to his right, so colorless and dull in comparison to the side of town he preferred. Others stared, but he didn't care what they thought or how ridiculous he appeared. This would be it—he could sense it—the piece that would alter the course of his life.

Then it all collapsed as he stumbled down onto the ground.

A female voice screeched as she, too, fell on top of him. He huffed, his cheek against the cobblestone. The woman profusely apologized, and the voice was familiar to him. She pushed herself off of him until she was standing. He rolled over onto his back. Up above them, Potek flew by. He squinted at the bird, and he could have sworn it squawked with laughter. The woman seemed to be too busy grumbling at herself to notice Potek, or his wings that changed color in mid-air.

Izyk focused back on the woman. At least this time she wasn't holding any papers.

"It's you," he said.

She sighed. "Again."

"It seems the Gods are telling us something."

"Yes, that we're both bad at paying attention."

"Or," he began, "that we are destined to be together."

"I don't think the Gods care about our romantic lives."

"I didn't say anything about romance," he crooned, and she rolled her eyes. "The Gods are strange." Izyk, now off the ground, wiped at the dirt on his pants and coat. "What possibly could have been occupying your mind again?"

"My work," she grumbled.

He gestured with his hands for her to elaborate. When she didn't, he asked, "Which is?"

"I'm one of this year's Undertaking inventors."

Oh. He hadn't expected that. She looked like she was dressed to attend a prestigious class, not work with her hands in a dark and dreary workshop.

"So the fate of our court rests on the shoulders of an inventor who is bad at walking."

"First..." She held up a finger. "You're as much to blame for our collisions as I am. Second," she lifted another long finger, this one adorned with a simple golden ring, "it doesn't entirely rest on me. There are four other participants, and the Heart just needs to pick one invention worthy enough for the Gods."

Izyk crossed his arms. "Our odds are still against us." She opened her mouth, but he stopped her before she could even bother defending herself—because an idea had formed, and unlike his tune from earlier, he knew he could hold onto it. "You're clearly struggling with finding an idea." She looked at him suspiciously, likely wondering how he could tell. Years of abandonment meant he was a great observer. "Those papers that flew around the market? I glimpsed some of your work. It looked like you had basic sketches, but nothing set in stone. The fact that you're so lost in your head? You're trying to find something around you to inspire a winning idea."

Her mouth hung open, and Izyk stepped closer. He took his finger under her chin and closed it for her.

"How dare you—"

"Am I wrong?"

Her shoulders sagged, and he almost felt guilty for calling out the truth.

"You're right," her voice cracked with the admission.

Oh no. He couldn't deal with tears. He'd had enough of those after his childhood. So instead, he had a proposition for her.

"Good thing I am here to help."

"What do you mean?"

The fact that she even entertained it showed her desperation.

"I need help, too."

She shook her head, and small strands of her brassy hair spilled from her tightly pulled-back hair. It must have loosened after the fall. "I don't have time to offer you. I need to focus on my work."

"You need to get out of that dark workshop and see the world."

She scoffed, but didn't insult him back. "What do you get in return?"

He clicked his tongue. "Correct me if I'm wrong, but there is a prize for winning the Heart. A subsidy from the court to show its thanks." Although Izyk always complained that the *last* people who needed money were the gifted.

"Yes…" she trailed, the realization dawning on her.

"I want a cut of it."

"To do what?"

"That's my business, Sparkling."

"I don't think—"

"Don't think," he said, shrugging nonchalantly. "Just act."

She swallowed hard, and he watched the bob of her throat. A flash of something sparked through her eyes, like the gold in them had a life of their own.

"Okay."

It had been hard to say no to those golden brown eyes, Piora thought to herself as she headed to the workshop. They had agreed to meet each other in two days time along the docks. He had plans for them already.

She didn't know what exactly she had agreed to; she just knew that perhaps he had some answers that she could not find on her own.

It was a risk to trust someone she didn't know, but…as scared as she might be, she could feel the lightning that coursed through her veins wanting to latch on to that stranger; he held some kind of power over her that she could not explain.

She didn't allow herself to ruminate on it for too long because she only had so many hours in a day, and right now, her priority was rifling through her sketches to determine if anything stood out.

"You look like you walked through the burial grounds in the middle of the night."

Piora jumped, clutching a hand to her chest at her friend's sudden greeting. The workshop had been quiet for the past hour, the rest of the inventors hard at work, so the sudden voice was akin to a boom of thunder.

"I just can't figure this out," Piora admitted. Most would deter her from being so open with her competitors. Everyone kept their inventions a secret until the day of the Undertaking to avoid anyone stealing ideas, but Piora was confident that she could trust Daria, and always felt better after voicing her concerns to her friend. "Nothing feels right."

Daria bent at the waist and rested her elbows on Piora's table. Her hair, with its pink strands that weaved through the braids, spilled over her shoulders. Cinnamon and sweet orange perfume wafted from Daria's skin, and the scent was comforting to Piora. "I think we're all struggling."

Piora wiped her forehead, suddenly finding herself too warm in the workshop.

"What if we all fail?"

Her friend shrugged. "It's never happened before." The whole court would be dead if that were the case, because the court's power wouldn't be replenished. "It's not impossible, but I think we have the talent here to please the Gods. One of us will succeed."

Piora wished she had the same amount of faith as her friend. Instead, there was a stifling fear that she was taking the place of someone who was better than her, someone whom the Gods had fated to win this year's Undertaking. Perhaps she should have listened to her calling as future minister because that is what the Weather Gods intended for her to do. Had she doomed the whole court by refusing that role?

Four

"**Y**ou're late," Izyk said.

He was lounging on a wooden bench, his arm stretching across the back, and his head tilted towards the gray skies. Rain would strike the land soon, Piora could feel it in her gut. Her powers wanted to escape the clutches of her body, to roam free with the storm.

With the strong gusts of wind, the sea raged, making it harder to hear each other. She stepped closer to him.

"I had to help my mom first." She didn't offer more than that.

He shrugged, as if he didn't actually care that she was later than the time they agreed on. "Let's go," he said as he stood up.

He wore a deep brown coat, a color matching his buzzed hair, allowing his eyes to stand out. Within the gloom, the golden brown almost appeared yellow, like two flashes of light guiding her.

They walked down the cobblestone path, passing by others who had their heads covered with their collars or scarves. Piora's own eyes watered at the whipping wind, but she pushed on. Sometimes, she considered running away to the Rain Court to escape the chill of the

Lightning Court, but then, she remembered how much she hated sand and stopped entertaining the idea.

"I never got your name," Izyk said as he rubbed his hands together. "I feel like that might help."

Piora hesitated, though she didn't know why. It's not like her name held meaning, but there was something intimate about sharing her name with a man like him, who looked like type of guy who didn't care for many people, but those he did, he held close.

"Piora," she offered.

"Piora," he repeated, extending the last syllable. From his mouth, the simple vowel sounded like a melody, and a chill rocked through her body. "A beautiful name."

Flustered, Piora pushed her shoulders back. "It's just a name."

"But it's *your* name," he said. "It holds part of your identity."

The seriousness of his tone made her uncomfortable. The weight he placed on something so insignificant only proved how much he romanticized trivial things.

"Are we close?" she deflected. She needed to redirect conversation.

"Nearly."

"And you can't tell me where we're heading?"

A mischievous smile crossed his face. "I want it to be a surprise. That first moment when it's revealed to you is important. It'll be where ideas will come pouring in from."

"You're so confident that this will work."

"Why would I try something with the expectation of failure?"

Piora's feet stopped on their own accord. She blinked at how easily the response came to him. She barely knew him, yet she could tell the way that he moved through life was so different.

"I guess I'm just the opposite of you when it comes to that. I always expect that things will go wrong."

Izyk rubbed his chin, where a hint of a beard began peeking through. She noticed the large array of rings spanning across all his fingers. She had the urge to ask about them, but held back as he said, "At least that mindset hasn't stopped you from trying."

Piora cocked a brow. "How do you know that?"

"Because you're here with me."

They trekked up the path into the woods, and even though it was chilly, sweat beaded along Piora's brow. Her legs were tired. She had spent most of her days sitting in front of a table with a light beaming in her face. The outdoors felt almost foreign to her. She pushed onward though; she wouldn't give Izyk a reason to tease her for her lack of stamina.

As if he knew she struggled, he said from his position in front of her, "We're almost there, Sparkling."

She grumbled at his use of the nickname. If she told him she didn't like it, he would use it nonstop, so she acted like she didn't care. Hopefully, over time, he would grow tired of the lack of response it earned him, and let it go. Though, with his mindset, he seemed to do whatever pleased him, even if it didn't go the way he expected.

She held on to a tree at a steep point, taking a big step upwards with her short legs. With every step, her own confidence in this being successful dwindled. Izyk's own seemed to heighten with the way he grunted in practical excitement, as if using the sound from his mouth to encourage his body to keep moving.

Piora needed a moment to rest. She bent down and clutched her hands over her knees as she tried taking deep breaths. The air had thinned out at this altitude.

She heard the continued crunching of twigs and leaves.

"You can't stop now," Iyk pestered her with a gentle smile on his face. His front teeth were crooked in an endearing way. She wondered about his past, what led him to music and this positive outlook. Did he ever have moments of doubt like she did? He seemed to approach life like he knew at every turn of the corner, there was something new and exciting and not something dreadful. She wished she could live the same way. His smile flattened slightly, and Piora turned away when she realized she was staring.

She inhaled deeply through her nose and exhaled slowly from her mouth, before she straightened, and began again.

His voice was gruff with pride, "That's my Sparkling."

Piora's eyes widened at the praise, but she didn't allow the shock to shake her up too much, even if she liked the way that sounded from his lips.

Finally, they made it to the top.

Izyk stopped and whipped around, which caused Piora to stumble and almost crash into him.

"What—"

"Prepare yourself, first. This is *the* moment we worked to get to. Make sure you can take it all in." He took out a pocket watch from inside his coat. "We have time, so no need to rush."

Once again, Piora found herself taking a deep breath. For some reason, a coil of nerves started in her stomach. There was a pressure there that she didn't appreciate.

"Let that worry go."

She snapped to look at him. "How do—"

"Your face shows it all."

She narrowed her eyes at him.

"Close your eyes," he commanded.

"What? No."

"Just do it. Trust me."

Piora hesitated for a split second, but then she relented too easily for her liking. What did she have to lose by following his orders?

A pressure weighed down on her shoulders. She tried to relax. Then, his hot breath blew on her ears as he said, "Roll them backwards"

She did as he bade. He let her lead the movements, but it was the feeling of his presence that calmed her even more. His hands trailed down the length of her arms, until they reached her hands. He held on to them, the metal of his numerous rings biting softly into her skin.

"I'm going to touch your neck now."

She nodded, practically hypnotized from his instructions. The warmth of his hands pressed against her neck. Her pulse quickened.

"Now, roll your head to your right." She did. "Your left." She did. "Slowly open your eyes."

Her lashes fluttered open and the first thing she noticed was the blush on his cheeks.

He gave her a cocky grin. "Better?"

She hated admitting it, but she did feel better. Her muscles felt like they could climb another hill if she really wanted to—though she didn't really want to.

His hands returned to his sides. "Let's go, then."

Watching Piora relax under his hands and hearing the soft, moany breaths from her lips had driven Izyk mad, and made him want to bring her closer to him. She became pliable under his command, and Izyk couldn't believe how easily she trusted him. He didn't complain, though. He loved how easily she went along with his instructions. It would make this challenge easier on them both.

He led the way, and taking the one last step up before they reached their destination, he breathed in the sight. Not of the sea crashing against the cliff they stood on—they were so high up, they were enshrouded in the clouds. No, he took in the sight of her.

Her mouth hung open, pure wonder there. Her cheeks were slightly red from the exertion of the hike, and the electricity in the air made strands of her hair stand up, almost like a halo. She looked like a goddess of lightning before him, standing upon her podium to the world.

Keeping quiet, he allowed her to take in the view, to not disturb that moment that could bring her the idea she was reaching for.

"I feel," she started, but stopped, hesitant. "I feel so connected to the Gods here. So close to nature and the oncoming storm."

Izyk squinted at the dark gray clouds that would soon roll in closer.

"The Gods might love to test us each year, but at least they know how to create a view," he joked.

She huffed a laugh, but didn't glance at him. She wandered closer and closer to the edge, one hand stretched out.

Sparks of lightning coated her fingertips, and the sky answered in response with its own flashes in the distance.

Jealousy burst in Izyk's chest, and he stamped it down, but it was hard to not let it come to fruition. He wanted those gifts, those powers that so easily came to her and others. A musician with gifts from the Gods would have had an easier time getting the coin he needed. Instead, he had been locked out of the prosperous side of society with the rest of the giftless. He hoped once he got the money from this deal, everything would change for him.

Piora took another step and gasped when her foot slid on soft earth, but Izyk grabbed her waist before she tumbled down to the rocks below.

"Careful, Sparkling," he said as he hoisted her back to safety. "Let's not return you to the Gods so soon."

She shook her head, as if coming out of a daze. "I don't even know what just happened. I just know I wanted to touch that lightning."

"Like I said, the Gods love their fun."

Pulling herself out of his arms, she turned to him. "But they would never intentionally put us in danger."

Izyk laughed harshly. When she didn't reciprocate, he turned serious. "Have you heard about the Undertaking in other courts?" When she didn't answer him, he continued. "In Thunder," he pointed towards the bordering court, "rocks rain from the skies. Many die. Snow? The Undertaking is a new challenge for every monarch, all of them deadly. I don't know why the Lightning Court's Undertaking is just a showoff of how the lightning powers can be used, but we are the lucky ones. Not everyone else is."

There was an additional weight to those words.

Piora's mouth clamped shut.

She must have had no idea. Her mother being the minister must have protected her from the harsh truth of the Gods. Though, from his travels and his own curiosity, he had learned the other courts weren't so divided between the gifted and the giftless—outside the Rain Court which occupied two worlds: one on land and the other in the sea. Perhaps, the true punishment of this court was just being born wrong.

"So..." he tried changing the subject. "Any new ideas for your invention?"

She took another glance to the horizon, where the storm clouds were racing closer. They could see the rain beginning to fall. The onslaught would soon be upon them.

"No."

He didn't let his disappointment show, only smiled. "Then I guess we'll be spending more time together."

"I guess so."

Just as they began their journey down, the rain reached them. Had he angered the Gods by revealing a part of their dark truth to the naïve hopeful before him? He didn't care. She deserved to know, and he refused to take it as a bad sign. He had no doubts: they both would end their little experiment successfully.

Five

The rain poured, and they slid down the hillside as they descended. Her clothes clung to her skin in a disgusting way, and all she wanted was to sit in front of a warm fire. Instead, she was battling for her life. She didn't want to fall down the mountain. Not only would it be painful and potentially deadly, but entirely embarrassing. She already felt dumb for her lack of knowledge on the other Undertakings. How could she have been so ignorant? How could she have never bothered learning about it? Her mother formed a bubble around her, and Piora had happily lived within its confines, not bothering to question life outside it.

"Watch out!" Izyk yelled from behind her.

She dug her toes into the ground before she hit the tree in front of her, her face scrunched as she pushed and prayed that she could stop her body as it propelled forward.

A hand wrapped around her arm, and she was yanked back.

"You're killing me here," he said over the pelt of the rain. "If I didn't know any better, I would think you like it when I save you."

She scoffed even though she had to admit his warmth. His large hand practically wrapped all the way around her bicep. No wonder he played so beautifully and fluidly on the piano—his fingers could easily stretch the length of the keys.

A burst of lightning flashed over them, and while his hand tightened over her, Piora savored its light.

"We should keep going," she told him. "It's going to get even darker soon."

He nodded, but he didn't let her go this time. They trudged through the trees and leaves and rocks together as the rain spilled over them. Her hair was beginning to get heavy on her head, but she couldn't stop now.

Once they got back to the town streets, it was deserted and quiet, even as the lamp posts glowed for anyone who dared brave the storm.

"This way," he urged her towards him, in the opposite direction of her home. "My home is just up the street. We can dry up there."

Piora paused, but the chill in her bones made the decision to follow him easy. A bright yellow bird swooped by them, so close that Izyk had to duck. He swore under his breath, and if Piora heard correctly, he chastised it. She would have to ask later because right now, she craved getting inside.

A burst of warmth hit them as they entered a tavern. Thankfully, it was empty.

Piora scrunched her brows in confusion, but Izyk quickly clarified. "My room is upstairs. We can stay here for now."

She stepped over to the hearth, where a fire merrily crackled. "Do you own this place?" she asked as she extended her hands towards the heat.

"No, but a friend does."

"Ah," she said. When her hands finally didn't feel frozen, she took off her coat. It was soaked through. She hung it on a chair to dry, but her sweater clung, uncomfortable and damp on her body. He must have noticed her inspecting the sweater because he came towards her.

"Let me bring you something dry," he urged, and stormed up the stairs before Piora could deny him.

When he returned, his coat was off. The wet, white shirt he wore was transparent, and she could see the hard muscles under it, the way they stretched as he offered her a dry sweater. She, on the other hand, stood awkwardly with her arms around herself.

She didn't want to change in front of him. He was a stranger. "I—"

"Do you want something to drink?" he asked, as he placed the sweater on the brown couch and turned towards the bar, giving her privacy.

She cleared her throat and she shrugged off her own sweater quickly to change. "Anything warm?"

He hummed to himself. "I can heat up some cider."

"Perfect."

She pulled the sweater over her head, then sat at the stool by the bar as he started up the stove. Taking the opportunity to finally bring down her hair, the strands fell in a swoop with the water weighing them down. She squeezed her hair, and water trickled to the floor. She would need to clean that up, along with the muddy trail she left with her shoes.

Piora scrubbed her scalp, relieving the tension of having her hair up so tight all day, then she did her best to comb through the tangled tresses with her fingers. Hissing at the pain, she quickly gave up.

"And here it is," Izyk said, turning with two steaming cups in his hands. "Oh," he paused. "Is that what you've been hiding from the world?"

Heat raced to her neck and cheeks. "I'm not hiding it. I'm just managing it in a way that best suits my life."

"Well, I'm jealous." He placed the cups down on the counter and pointed to his buzzed hair.

"Don't be. It's an absolute nuisance."

"But, think of all the fun," he said dreamily, as he rested his elbow on the bar. "I would whip it in people's faces as I walked by them, completely unapologetic."

She snorted into the hot and sweet beverage, the taste delightful to her tongue. "My mother despises that I don't wear it down all the time, like her. But she doesn't understand that lightning and long hair don't exactly mesh."

"Especially for someone as clumsy as you."

Piora gave him a sharp look, but ignored the jibe. "And she refuses to let me cut it. So, up it goes."

He came to sit beside her on a neighboring stool, but instead of facing the bar, his legs were angled towards her. "I always say, comfort over beauty."

An easy thing for him to tout when he looked like he was forged from the Gods themselves.

"I also think," he added, as he took a large gulp from his own cup—how he downed the hot beverage like that, she didn't know—"you have a right to do whatever you want with your hair, even cut it off."

She picked at the end of her hair that waved slightly. "I've contemplated it...cutting it off, that is. But something keeps pulling me back."

"The pressure of disappointing others."

She snapped her attention to him, surprised by his accurate assessment. "That doesn't seem fair."

Tapping the wooden bar, he said, "It's the truth though, right? That's why you're bent on winning the Undertaking, to prove that you are worthy to yourself, your mother, and the Gods."

She suddenly slid off the stool, readying herself to go. She didn't like the words coming out of his mouth, and how easily he seemed to understand her when he barely knew her.

But he was at her side before she could even step away, caging her against the bar. "You're still wet. You'll get sick if you leave like this."

She gulped. He was so much taller than her, yet she wasn't frightened of those intense eyes that glowed against the fire.

Ducking her head, she stared behind his shoulder. "I'm sorry—"

"Don't apologize," he sighed. "If you really want to leave, you can. As I said, you can do whatever you like." He pulled away, but Piora pushed her back further into the wood of the bar.

When she didn't move, he stared at her, anticipating. She bit her lip, and he tracked the movement with his eyes, his eyes that were becoming more black than golden brown as his pupils dilated.

"What if I don't know what I want," she barely managed to breathe out, her heart racing.

His boot thudded closer to her. "Perhaps I can show you." Izyk bent down towards her, and Piora lifted her head up, her eyes open, taking in his beauty.

Their lips barely brushed together, and immediately, electricity poured from inside her. He steadied his hands on the bar again as she grasped at his wet shirt. He pressed closer to her.

She flattened her palms against his abdomen, and his muscles flexed, as his tongue gently coaxed her mouth open while the taste of apple and whisky consumed her. Her body felt as it had when she had stood upon that cliff and the lightning flashed, the same connection of power and otherworldliness—like she both belonged on the ground and in the sky. She floated, rising on her toes, bending her neck further back to give him better access.

She heard the wood of the bar groan as she licked the roof of his mouth, teasing him. Piora was lost in him, and she didn't know if she would find her way back.

Then, someone cleared their throat. At first, she thought it was the Gods themselves, but when Izyk stopped and she finally opened her eyes, she saw another gentleman on the stairs.

"I hope I'm not disrupting." A mischievous smile broke across the man's lips, his long beard following the movement of his mouth. He looked middle-aged, with faint lines beginning to form across his forehead and around his eyes.

Izyk rested his forehead against hers. "We'll be done shortly, Ludwik."

Ludwik chuckled, and he crept back up the stairs.

"I should probably go—" she started.

"I'll grab your coat," he said.

They stared at each other again, and Izyk's swollen lips and large eyes bore into her soul. She wondered if she appeared much the same.

"Meet me again next week," Izyk said, quick and disheveled, as if worried that if he didn't say the words now, he never would. "Same time, but here instead."

Piora nodded because words failed her right now. She grabbed her things and left the bar. The rain had slowed to a drizzle, but the only sensation that mattered was the taste of him that lingered in her mouth.

Izyk slammed down the mug after tossing back what remained of his tepid cider. He could still feel the touch of her gentle hands on him, the way they had explored his abdomen and chest as he flicked his tongue in her mouth, as she arched into him.

"I hope you know what you're doing," Ludwik said from his spot on the stairs again.

"And if I told you I didn't?"

"Then I would call you a bastard for roping in that innocent woman."

Izyk scoffed. "She's an adult like the both of us, she could have easily said no or asked me to stop."

His friend leaned over against the bar, smelling her cup. When he was satisfied there was no alcohol in hers, but disgusted when he smelled it on Izyk's breath, Ludwik finally responded. "You know it's not that easy to just say no."

"I would never push her," Izyk snapped.

"Of course you wouldn't, you're too kind-hearted—but she doesn't know that."

Izyk grunted, but appreciated how empathetic his friend was. He supposed it made sense with what happened to his sister years ago; how her husband had changed once the ring was on her finger, how he forced himself on her until she ended up hurt. Ludwik had found her outside his bar, bloody and unconscious. Apparently, the man had been angry that she had lost the Undertaking, and thus their chance at a better life with the earnings she could have made. After she healed, she left for the Rain Court, leaving Ludwik to take care of her son until he was old enough to join his mother. At least the two were now together. But that paternal instinct hadn't left Ludwik, which made him the perfect owner of this tavern.

"So where exactly did you find her?" Ludwik asked curiously.

"She's minister Kaplana's daughter."

Ludwik choked on his drink, some of the liquid sputtering into his long, brown beard. "What are you doing with *her*?"

Izyk shrugged as he poured himself another drink, this time straight liquor. He would need to pay for all this, he knew, with coin he couldn't afford to lose, but he needed the comfort of the liquid's burn.

"Helping her."

His friend shook his head in disbelief. "With what?"

"She's one of the Undertaking inventors this year, and she needs inspiration for her creation."

"And your tongue can offer that?"

Unimpressed with his friend's line of questioning, Izyk sat by the fire. "If she wins, then she'll split the money with me."

"And you are one step closer to buying the music hall."

"I wouldn't be just a step closer, I could buy it outright."

Ludwik poured his own drink. "Your problems can all be fixed by this one girl."

"Not all. I'm still trying to write the perfect piece that will draw crowds to even want to attend any performances that I put on."

"Who knows," Ludwik started with a cheeky smile on his face. "Her tongue might just inspire *you*."

Izyk snorted, but then he looked down into his half empty cup and remembered his lips on hers, the way he had itched to touch her hair but had held back; and most noticeably, the lightning that he felt pulsing under her skin, and how he wanted to see it come out and touch him. There was so much power nestled in her small body, yet he could tell that she didn't understand the depth of it by the way she spoke of her mother and how she easily listened to others, instead of acting of her own free will.

He knew now that breaking down that wall would be the answer to how she discovered what she wanted—*needed*—to invent.

"And what does she think about what you desire to do with the money?"

"She doesn't know."

"You care for her," Ludwik assumed, a wild accusation to claim when Izyk knew only the bare details of the woman.

"I care about the music hall."

"No," his friend pushed back. "You care about her. I can see it."

"Let's not get romantic. We're both just giving each other what we need to accomplish what we set out to do."

Izyk couldn't see it, but he could sense that Ludwik was rolling his eyes.

"You may be talented and motivated, but sometimes you can be too foolish for your own good."

Izyk didn't let those words settle into his chest. He wouldn't allow it. He had one ultimate goal here, and he wouldn't lose track of it. His feelings for Piora couldn't get in the way.

Six

Piora couldn't face her mother right now, so she decided to head to the workshop instead. Luckily, darkness greeted her as she entered. She turned the switch and the lights pulsed to life, the thrum of electricity jolting her to the present.

Her workstation was disorganized, as it usually was. She didn't have the right mindset to actually work right now, but she sat on the cold metal chair and stared at the space, her eyesight going blurry.

She couldn't believe what had transpired between her and Izyk, how she had so easily become hypnotized by his smell and touch and taste—how she never wanted to stop feeling his mouth on hers. Worst of all, how she wanted his lips to trail over her entire body, his fingers to brush through her hair, until her powers crackled to the surface and she shone like a glittering star for him.

She blinked and shook off the direction of her thoughts. With such limited time before the Undertaking, she needed to focus on her invention. Although she didn't want to say today was a waste of time, she couldn't say it was the most useful.

Piora had to admit that being on that cliff, watching the lightning, had revitalized her and reminded her exactly why she wanted to win the Undertaking. Perhaps Izyk had been right. She wanted to prove her worth to the Gods, and she found nothing wrong with that. The Gods had blessed them with their world, and she planned to deliver an invention that showed her gratitude for it.

Unfortunately, as she flipped through her sketches *again*, her shoulders sank at the disappointment of her own ideas. A device that would blow warm air so that hair could be dried faster—useful for someone like her, with locks so long it took hours for the dampness to evaporate, but someone like Izyk would never need it. She would be excluding many with such a device, and she didn't feel the Gods would favor it as a result. Then, she brushed her fingers over the lines of the blueprint for an object that would zap small bugs and kill them instantaneously. Piora winced at what the Gods would think about her creating a device of death, even for tiny, annoying creatures.

"I am useless," she whispered to herself.

"I mean, you're not wrong…"

Piora fell out of her chair and slammed onto the ground, hitting her elbow on the way down. She winced in pain, but quickly recovered as she stood up to identify the intruder.

Or, worse—a fellow inventor.

"What are you doing here, Roksana?"

Roksana crossed the room, her generous curves swaying as she did. "Same as you. Trying to get ahead so I can win this thing."

Piora gulped. Roksana always had such a commanding presence in a room that she caused others to balk, and Piora was not immune to that.

Roksana flipped her brown waves over her shoulders and a waft of something floral flooded Piora's nose. It wasn't unpleasant, just an attack on her senses.

"I have so many great ideas, but am having such trouble deciding which to choose." Roksana pouted her perfect red lips, as if she had just reapplied the color only minutes ago. "Professor Silo and I narrowed it down to two, but the final call is impossible."

Piora wished that was her problem, but she wouldn't admit that aloud. Ultimately, Roksana was her competitor, and she didn't want to reveal how far behind she felt in comparison.

"I'm sure you'll pick the best one from your arsenal of ideas," Piora said.

Roksana sighed dramatically. "I hope so. I want to make sure the Gods see how invaluable I am."

"The Gods already think you are invaluable." At least that's what Piora's mother had told her—that everyone was purposefully placed in their respective courts for a reason, even the ungifted. Piora hated that her mother used that word though, and she hated it even more when she described Piora as double gifted, a sign that she was meant to lead this court as the minister once her mother's own tenure came to an end.

With her mother's logic, Piora always wondered how she ended up in the Lightning Court, why she was destined for it. Piora was haunted to learn how violent and dangerous the Undertakings were in other courts. Piora couldn't imagine being in the Thunder Court, and having rocks fall down on her, or in the Snow Court, where all the pressure landed on a single Royal. It was a shivering revelation.

"We all know that isn't true," Roksana said with a derisive tone. "One of us will be worthy enough of the Heart, and will be the reason that the court's power is replenished. The others will be either forgotten or labeled as losers. I refuse to let my fate come to that."

The reminder of that truth churned Piora's gut until she felt like she needed to sit, but she didn't let it show. Though, Roksana had a point. Those who did not win the Heart were forgotten. She couldn't remember ever meeting another participant before. Was it shame that held them back from admitting their pasts, or something worse? Piora refused to dwell on it. She had other worries.

"We are all worthy," Piora said with little conviction, because she herself didn't believe those words. How could she when she was competing for validation of her own worthiness? "The Gods will choose wisely. They will choose whose invention they deem the most useful for the court. We have to trust them."

Roksana inspected Piora, her teal-blue eyes flicking up and down as she crossed her arms over her sizable chest. "Let's hope the Gods actually follow through on that."

Piora watched Roksana grab her black leather bag from her station and leave. She didn't understand why Roksana doubted the Weather Gods so much. Ever since the creation of the courts and the start of the Undertakings, they had chosen fairly. Why would this year be different?

Izyk wore his best clothes, which wasn't anything special, but this was an important meeting for him. He wouldn't let anything jeopardize it.

He entered the bank, his shoes squeaking against the polished oak wood floors. Blysk, the banker responsible for the music hall, sat at his desk, his head bent down as he squinted at a collection of papers. His gray hair was pulled back with wax, revealing his large forehead, age spots, and wrinkles that showcased both his wisdom and short temper.

Izyk pulled out the chair without asking permission. The noise startled Blysk, but he glowered at Izyk when he noticed who had caused the loud disruption.

"Unless you have every coin and copper needed to pay for the music hall, this meeting is pointless," Blysk said without looking up from whatever was capturing his attention. "And I doubt you have it."

"Such little confidence, Blysk." Izyk tsked, propping his feet up on the desk. "I'm offended."

"And you offend me," Blysk spat the words as he wiped away the dirt from Izyk's shoes that had landed on his pristine desk.

Unlike his counterpart next to him, whose space was chaotic, colorful, and with character—more Izyk's style—Blysk's workspace seemed hollow.

"I have good news," Izyk continued, picking up a quill from the man's desk. Blysk rejected any progress made by the inventors. Although Izyk was also slow to accept change, he could put his pride aside to use an ink pen—those at least made life easier. "I'm going to have the money for you just after the Undertaking."

It might be premature, but he had no doubt Piora would win. He wouldn't tell Piora that he was here and that he held such confidence—not yet, anyway—because he knew she would react poorly. But he lived his life in a way where he anticipated everything working out in his favor.

"Oh?" Blysk paused, his attention finally turning Izyk's way. "And who is being so charitable?"

"You don't actually care where the money is coming from, as long as you get it, so what does it matter?"

"I care," he enunciated, the hard sound a crisp, "if you're attaining the coin from some criminal activity."

"You know I'm honorable."

Blysk crossed his hands on top of the desk, clearly growing impatient. "Izyk, I know nothing about you, except your pointless desire for an old building that is years away from crumbling."

Blysk exaggerated; the building was still sturdy and would outlast both Blysk and Izyk if taken care of properly. For someone who held onto the past like Blysk, he assumed the man would have adoration for the abandoned part of town. Unfortunately, Blysk was blessed with a morsel of lightning, enough that allowed him to protect people's accounts and to scare any of the giftless from trying to steal from this bank. Since he was considered gifted, he didn't care about what happened to the giftless, hence his obvious animosity towards Izyk and his desperate dreams.

Izyk leaned forward. "I'm getting you that money, so please make sure to not sell the place to anyone else or allow it to be destroyed before then."

"I don't answer to you. We are all aware of the timeline. Lucky for you, the deadline for someone buying it is after the Undertaking, so I'll be here waiting."

Blysk's attention sunk back into his paperwork, like he didn't care at all, which he clearly didn't, but Izyk had hoped to see a spark of excitement. It was a big deal. That building had been empty for too long. Finally, because of him, because of his desperate fight, the court would have music once again, with a sacred place to cherish it.

Nothing would stop him now.

Seven

Piora spent the morning with her eyes straining at her sketchbook, the gloomy day and the bright yellow light of the workstation creating a painful contrast. Attempting to relieve some of the growing tension, she released sparks of her lightning against the metal table, the power bouncing up and down like a ball before it sizzled away into nothing.

When she arrived home yesterday—thankfully, mostly dry—her mother had taken one look at her and knew that something had occurred that she disapproved of. Piora barely made it a step inside before her mother was hounding her with numerous questions about her day.

Piora made an excuse that she had gotten busy at the workshop, and then caught in the rain. However her mother then asked about the smell of fire and apples clinging to her clothes. Piora had forgotten she was still wearing Izyk's sweater.

Piora told a half-truth: that she ducked into a random tavern to dry off and warm up while she let the storm ease. Her mother squinted her eyes, clearly incredulous, but let it go as soon as she noticed how Piora was beginning to shiver. Piora's mother pushed her towards the small fire and drew her a warm bath, refusing to let Piora get sick.

Now, Piora anticipated whatever Izyk had planned for her. She was scared that nothing would come of this, scared of disappointing him. He clearly needed the money. What if she failed to provide it? They both would have wasted their time.

"You always look like someone just died," Daria said, evidently on her way out, with her bag on her shoulders.

Piora straightened. "And you always have a smile on your face. I'm jealous."

Her friend shrugged. "I'm grateful for what I have and the opportunity to be able to participate in the Undertaking."

"There are only so many people within the court who could even participate, though. The probability of getting chosen is high if you enter."

Anyone between the ages of twenty-two and twenty-eight could enter their name if they wanted, and they could do it every year until reaching the maximum age, as long as they hadn't already participated. At twenty-three, Piora was picked on her second try. Daria was only a year older.

"Those chances aren't as high as you think when you think about the corruption going on."

Piora cocked her head. "What corruption?"

"How some pay to have their name entered multiple times to increase their chances."

"My mother handles the lottery. She would never tolerate that." Piora scoffed at such a notion. As frustrating as her mother was, she was honorable.

"Where do you think the winner's money comes from each year?"

"There's a small fee to enter…"

"That wouldn't be enough for the high reward this court likes to give," Daria corrected. "Your mother, I'm sure, gladly accepts the bribes and keeps any extra for herself."

Piora didn't know why she was defending her mother, but she did. "My mother would never. The Gods would disavow such behavior."

"I don't think they would. The Weather Gods are just as corrupt. Look at how they watch us struggle just to please them so we don't die. We might not have to face terrorizing monsters, but each year, this court has the stress about its potential downfall."

"But—"

"Just look at your home in comparison to others, Piora. It's as large as the chapel."

She supposed Daria had a point, but surely, there was another explanation.

"Ask your mother. Though, I have a feeling she wouldn't be honest if you did."

Daria wasn't wrong. Asking her mother, accusing her of stealing money, would end in disaster. Piora took that information to the side and closed it up for now. She would deal with it later, when the Undertaking was over and she could focus again.

But now, more than ever, she wanted to win so that she could give the coin to Izyk, because she didn't need it like he so clearly did.

"You seem nervous."

Izyk watched as Piora wrung her hands together and stared out into nothing.

Her attention snagged on him finally as she said, "I just learned some information that surprised me today."

"Care to divulge the news?"

She shook her head, her eyes glazed with a tired haunt. He didn't push her, and instead changed the subject to the reason they were both in Ludwik's tavern again.

"Are you ready?"

She nodded, more enthusiastically now. "Where are we going?"

"Nowhere."

Her lips thinned and her pointed nose scrunched. "We're staying here? That doesn't sound too exciting."

Ludwik coughed from where he was wiping down the tables and serving a few patrons getting in an early drink to drown their woes.

She winced and apologized.

"We're leaving," he clarified. "Just not going anywhere."

"You're contradicting yourself."

He let out an exasperated sigh. "We're taking a walk." At her hesitance, he added, "When was the last time you took a walk with no destination in mind?"

He could see the question churning in her mind, as she finally responded, "Never. I always have somewhere to be."

"Exactly." He stuck his finger up to prove his point. "If you love the Gods so much, then you should make time to appreciate what they created."

She shook her head and rolled her eyes at him, but her casual annoyance quickly turned to a serene acceptance. The flip of her emotions was so quick, most would likely miss it. Not Izyk—he had his eyes on her.

He opened the door and gestured for her to go ahead. The rain had thankfully stopped, but a cold frost from the sea had come through, and the lack of sun kept away any warmth.

At least Piora had bundled up. Her hands remained in her pockets as they strolled down the street.

"Don't be afraid to stop if something catches your eye. We have no goal, so let your eyes wander, and your heart take you where it wants."

"Why would I be afraid?" she asked as she stopped in the middle of the cobbled road. Someone bumped into her as they tried to pass, and *she* apologized.

Izyk rubbed at the back of his neck, his warm coat uncomfortable as she gazed at him. Did he want to expose the truth of her? Yes, he did.

"You don't like to inconvenience anyone, and you think stopping will do just that. But," he started before she could open her mouth to retort. "That's not possible when I, too, have nowhere I need to be."

"Shouldn't you be trying to earn money for whatever you need it for?"

He hadn't gone busking in the market or taken on any more gigs since their agreement. Ludwik had noticed and called Izyk foolish for having such strong faith in someone he didn't even know.

"I need inspiration too, remember? Performing new songs always gets a crowd and more coin," he said. It was an excuse, though not entirely a lie. He still hadn't written the perfect piece that he wanted to debut at the grand re-opening of the music hall. That day, when the lights would be back on, when an entire orchestra played with him, he wanted the place to shine brighter than the lightning of Elektra, herself. He wanted to dazzle the audience until they wondered how they have could ever let such a beautiful building lay abandoned for so long.

"Right..."

"Let's keep going."

"I thought you said I lead, you follow."

His mouth gaped open, but then he smiled, his teeth showing. "Of course, Sparkling. Let us stand here and wait for the large crowds going to the market to stampede us."

She looked behind her, and he saw the moment of realization. The market would be opening soon, and there was always a rush to get there first.

Without a word, she turned around and led the way.

Eight

Unfamiliar roads surrounded Piora. She always took the same routes to get to the workshop, her home, the chapel, or the shops. She never found a reason to venture outside of the most efficient ways of getting somewhere. Today, though, with the wind whipping from the sea and Izyk beside her, she didn't think as she went.

The outskirts of this town had become abandoned, old wooden buildings rotted, dried ivy wrapped around them that crumbled with the smallest gust. She wondered who used to occupy these homes, who owned the shops. She wondered what happened to them now.

They looped around, heading back towards the town center where streets bustled with life again, the buildings turned to a gray brick, and the lamp posts actually worked.

She noticed the small things, too. The rain that was still stuck in the cracks of the road and how it glistened against the streetlights. The way each block took her around fifty steps. How some lights were a warmer tone and others cooler, depending on the inventor and their unique lightning power.

What she noticed the most, though, was Izyk. He walked behind her the whole time, letting her lead as he promised, but she caught him checking his pocket watch a few times, which made her anxious. Did he have somewhere to be? Was he lying to her?

She kept quiet about it, not allowing that to distract her from the entire point of this walk. She assumed it was a nervous tick, something to do with whatever he needed the money for. The urge to ask about it again came up, but she ignored it, forcing herself to not let her life and others get in the way of the task at hand.

One of the window displays called to her, and she pressed her nose against the glass, her hot breath creating condensation. A vast array of trinkets were scattered across different shelves, some old books, too.

Izyk stopped next to her and bent down to inspect a ceramic statuette of a small quartet of frogs playing instruments. They were dressed in fine attire, with different colored bow ties. The craftsmanship was beautiful.

"That's fun," she commented, needing to dispel the silence.

He hummed, his lips quirking to one side, as if unsure. "Not my style, but it's unique and hand-made at least. Not like those boring inventions that all look the same."

Piora didn't know what to make of that statement. "I didn't realize you were so against the gifts that the inventors provide."

"Not against. There is value to the inventions, some even are life-saving. I just—" He bit down on his bottom lip before starting again. "I just think we are losing the beauty of humanity sometimes with them. Our lives have become easier, meaning we rely less on each other and lose connection."

"Making life easier is a *good* thing," she pushed. "And not everyone has people that they can rely on."

A rough chuckle escaped his lips. "I know, more than you think."

"Well I think the beauty is that we can have the pleasures of both. These objects, and the inventions, are created from the hearts and minds of people who care."

"Care about winning the money."

She shook her head. "The monetary reward wasn't always a part of it. It's something we as a court added less than half a century ago. Plus, I like to believe that the Gods wouldn't think an invention created just for the sake of staking a claim to the prize would be worthy of winning."

"Your faith in them is strong."

Piora turned on her side to lean against the window and get a better look at Izyk. "I grew up with my mother as minister, so it was indoctrinated in me from a young age."

"Too bad you weren't given the magic of the Sight like your mother. You'd be a great successor to the role."

Piora gulped, turning her attention back on the window before he could read her too closely. For some reason, she got the hint that revealing that she *could* take over for her mother, that the Gods had blessed her with two gifts—even though she refused to utilize one—would not bode well for her. Izyk clearly resented that he had no powers.

"We should keep going," she said, before he started prying too closely where she didn't want to follow.

He didn't need further encouragement. They continued on together, and his warmth radiated towards her. She stopped herself from stepping too close. They couldn't have a repeat of what had transpired last time. He was a dangerous distraction, and as much as she was tempted to act on what she craved, she wouldn't. Once she won the Undertaking and he had his coin, they would diverge onto their own paths again because he would no longer need her. So...she decided to protect herself for when that time came. They needed to keep it strictly professional.

It was always the same dream; her body splayed on a metal table, arms and legs bound, while attached wires hummed with the power of electricity. She wore the minister's white robes, though they felt constrictive, and less like a protective shield against what she knew was coming.

Piora didn't pull against the ropes anymore. As a child, she would struggle until her wrists became raw. As she tried to unchain herself from whatever was connected to those wires, she would feel pricks of sparks against her skin, shooting pain seizing and tensing the muscles beneath. The panic would swell within her until her snot dribbled down her nose, unable to wipe it away. Even as she screamed, tiring herself out, no one came to help.

So she learned how resigning herself to the fate of the dream was the best route. Letting the quiet and the stillness of the room fade, Piora squeezed her eyes and hands tightly shut, anticipating the next vision the Gods intended to show her.

Piora opened her eyes and stared down at the lifeless body of her mother, the once flush color of her face now gone, her usual bright blonde hair, dimmed.

With the court's minister dead, the Gods required a replacement. Even though just her and her mother were here, behind the haziness of the dream, all eyes were on her.

Piora didn't say anything, simply looked at the woman, at the person who had brought her to this world. Flashes of light sparkled around her, coming in and out, waiting for her to answer—like the Gods themselves had determined this would finally be when Piora submitted to what they had destined for her. Instead, she stayed perfectly still.

Piora was pushed into the next part of the dream, where she stood at the altar of the chapel, a congregation waiting to listen. Piora tirelessly stared back. She understood these Gods now. She would not utter a word to damn herself. The less she responded, the more bored they would become of these games and let her free again.

And when she expected to be dragged to another pointless scene, Piora woke up gasping.

Piora clutched her hands to her chest to remind herself that she was alive, the beat of her heart rapid underneath her ribs—there and whole.

The Gods never spoke to her in those dreams—they didn't need to, she supposed. They were able to get their message across seamlessly with what they put her through each time. They were becoming more incessant; these dreams happened almost every week. But Piora wouldn't give in, not even if she lost the Undertaking, not even if her mother pushed and pushed. If that happened, she would run away to another court. Perhaps, the Snow Court needed someone like her.

But she hoped her life wouldn't come to that. She leveraged Izyk's optimism as she told herself winning the Undertaking would solve her problems. Then she would be free to live the life she wanted. It was that simple.

Nine

"They're becoming more frequent, aren't they?"

Piora startled at her mother's sudden words, almost dropping the cup of tea she carried towards the table.

Before Piora could explain, her mother chided, "The Gods wouldn't bother you like this if you only listened to what they were saying."

Piora set the cup down before her anger spiraled. It was too early for this conversation, one they had many times before, and one whose outcome never changed. She considered abandoning her freshly brewed tea and the warm bread she spent all morning baking to avoid a rehash. But her mother prevented that from happening as she sliced her own piece of bread and spread jam over it, and brought it to the table.

Piora understood that meant that she wanted them to eat together. Her mother had complained how the amount of time they spent together had become less and less, even though that was the case because her mother had become too busy.

"Was it the same dream as usual?

Piora relented and sat down because she felt she had no other choice. She nodded, taking a bite of the bread. "Same sequence, too."

"Don't allow that to scare you. My dreams are always pleasant now. The Gods want to see you fulfill what they had planned for you."

"Then why give me the power of lightning?" Piora challenged.

Her mother's expression became stony, an anger radiating from her. "Perhaps to test your devotion. Will you be tempted by the glory and wonder of lightning or understand the beauty of the quiet Sight?"

Piora didn't think that was fair. Why must she be tested at all?

"A minister with lightning magic seems like a waste," Piora explained.

Her mother chewed on her bread and nonchalantly revealed, "You'd lose your lightning magic."

"What?" Piora coughed, as she swallowed her tea and it went down wrongly.

Her mother sipped her tea slowly as if she hadn't just dropped such big news. "The Gods would not allow you to do both, to *be* both. If you commit to participating in this Undertaking, you will lose the Sight. If you let go of your foolish desires and follow through with what you are meant to do, you will lose the lightning."

"How do you know?"

"Because I have the Sight. The Gods have shown me both outcomes."

Piora could guess they didn't show her mother which outcome would materialize to reality. But...she still didn't let that truth sway her to move forward with being a minister. Giving up the dreams from the Gods sounded better than ideal. Her lightning was what mattered, what she could do with it mattered for the betterment of the entire court.

"I could see you don't mind giving up your Sight, but they also showed me that if you lose, your lightning powers will dwindle over time, and you will become giftless."

Piora almost choked again. "What—Why?" she stammered, barely able to breathe.

To her knowledge, that had never happened before. No one permanently lost their powers if they lost the Undertaking, right? That would be a cruel fate from the Gods. The court needed all inventors and all those with lightning to continue working, to keep the lights on, to make sure inventions continued to function. That was always Piora's goal, even if she lost.

Her mother shrugged. "It is the will of the Weather Gods. Who am I to question them?"

"My options are then to either become the minister or risk losing my powers?"

"Yes."

"And you didn't tell me this sooner?"

"You were adamant about participating."

"So why tell me now?"

"Now...well, now I know that you are struggling, that you are wasting your time with some man instead of working. Maybe you won't be so stubborn anymore."

Piora shook her head, confused at how her mother knew that. "Are you having me watched?"

"The Gods are always watching."

Piora stormed out the door without a coat and without a care for anything. She sped towards the workshop, needing to head somewhere safe and familiar to expel the electric energy of the powers beginning to build up inside her.

She weaved through the streets, pushing by people who walked too slowly, and she didn't apologize for any of it, her surroundings a blur of grays and browns.

When her eyes began to burn, tears threatening to spill, she picked up her pace and ran. Her lightning charged in her chest. Her hands began to sizzle and spark unwillingly. She tried to rein it in but failed as a shot of it burst free. It blasted the wet road, glistened, then evaporated into nothing.

She heaved as she bent forward, her hands on her knees, trying to stamp down the tears, but failing miserably.

"You live up to your name, Sparkling."

Piora whipped her head to Izyk who leaned against exterior of the tavern, his arms and legs crossed.

Piora didn't realize she had been heading this way. The workshop was in the opposite direction. How did she not notice?

Izyk appeared unruffled by her, though, as if he was expecting her.

"What's got you so worked up?"

She wiped her nose before fully straightening and facing the man before her, one who she had already become so used to having in her life. Stupid and dangerous.

"The Undertaking," she told a half-truth. He didn't need to know the full extent of her problems, nor the harrowing relationship with her mother.

"Aren't we all always a bit nervous about that? What if this is the cohort to finally fail?"

"Is there something wrong with *you*? I've never heard you be so negative," she teased, turning the subject of the conversation on him. It was better than addressing the panic sizzling beneath her skin.

He pushed off the wall of the tavern, his footsteps slow and steady as he stalked towards her. "Trying out the pessimism to see why you like it so much." Izyk wiped at his wool coat—today a bright red—as if there were flecks of negativity there. "I don't like it."

Another zap of her power extinguished itself from her body, and it was like a sigh of relief, a knot of tension that had finally unravelled.

"Feel better?" he asked.

She didn't know. Partly yes, but there was a deeper ache that couldn't be fixed by Izyk's presence. She nodded, though, giving him the answer he wanted.

Izyk pulled her hair gently towards him, his fingers trailing smoothly through the tresses. In her rush, she hadn't tamed it in her typical style. She peered up at him, and his eyes had darkened.

"I didn't get to touch it last time," he said.

Flashes of them inside the tavern blinked before her eyes; the way his body caged hers, the gentleness of his lips before they turned fierce and hungry, how safe she had felt.

She didn't allow herself to get caught up in the memories. She readied to pull away, when a large squawk frightened her back. His fingers tugged at her hair, some strands plucked out of her scalp.

A green bird landed on Izyk's shoulder, and the fibers of his coat shifted to match the bird's emerald hue.

Izyk sighed. "Ignore him. I have no food, Potek." Izyk showed his empty hands to the bird.

Piora's mouth fell open as Potek nipped at Izyk's ear, as if searching for food hidden in there, completely ignoring Iyk's statement. Izyk ducked away, trying to get the bird to stop, but it refused, its wings flaring in frustration.

Unable to fully grasp the sight of what transpired in front of her, she continued their earlier conversation as Izyk fought against Potek still.

"I told you my hair is a nuisance. Anyway, I was just in a rush, and didn't have time to put it up, and somehow—"

"No need to get defensive, Sparkling. I was just stating a fact. I find it quite atrocious," Izyk said because right at that moment, the bird stilled. He seemed to want to listen to their conversation.

She crossed her arms. "I find you quite distasteful myself."

"Oh?" he crooned. "The woman bites." Potek, once again, attempted to poke at Izyk, but he shrugged the bird off until it was flying away. A few passerby watched in awe as the bird's feathers shifted colors right in front of their eyes.

She snorted. "I do when someone is being a nuisance. Clearly, Potek and I—."

"I bother you that much?"

"Stop interrupting me!"

Piora watched as Izyk staggered back, shocked at her outburst.

"I'm sorry."

"No." He shook his head. "Don't apologize." Then a strange smile crossed his face. "You're right. I do interrupt you, and you should call me out. You should have done it a long time ago."

"I didn't mean to yell."

"I liked it."

"Of course you would."

"What can I say? I'm predictable." A shiver rocked through her body as a chilly breeze blew against her face, reminding her she wasn't wearing a coat. Izyk finally noticed, too. "We should go inside."

"I should go to the workshop."

"I don't think any ideas are going to flow in your current state. A nice, warm cider with whisky should do the trick."

Not that Izyk didn't feel bad for her rough state, but watching Piora lose herself in her powers had been one of the most alluring experiences of his life. At one point, every inch of her sparkled and he wanted to touch her, to let that magic flow on to him so he could know what it was like to be gifted.

He held back, mainly because Potek decided to make an appearance, but also because riling Piora up would help ground her again. Having her yell at him stirred something in him, too. He hadn't realized how much he spoke over her, but he would work to listen; one would think a musician would know how to do that.

And her hair...it was like a brassy, antique gold, one weathered with time, but one that, even after years of use, was still beautiful.

Piora immediately headed straight towards the fire and kneeled on the fur rug—the sight had his heart swelling. A few other patrons loitered the room, still here from the night before, but Piora didn't seem to notice or care.

He took a seat on the couch behind her and observed how she just stared and stared into the heat, her breaths now even and shallow. He wondered how she had been become so hardened, and why she kept that anger leashed.

Ludwik came up behind him and whispered to Izyk. "I saw her little display outside. She better not bring that in here, and don't you dare even consider giving her a lick of alcohol."

Izyk waved off his friend. "She wouldn't. And I won't."

"She's fragile right now. She's unpredictable."

"I can control myself," Piora said from her spot, voice clear. "I will not set this place alight." Her eyes stayed on the fire as she spoke.

"See?" Izyk smiled, for some reason proud of her. "She's fine."

Ludwik's eyes switched between the both of them, assessing them harshly. "Just don't scare my customers. They're tired and too drunk for excitement."

"We can't promise you that," Izyk yelled to his friend as he left.

Piora snorted, and he liked when he could make her laugh.

After Izyk got them their drinks, they sipped in silence. He could tell Piora needed to work out what was in her head alone. Then, he would ask her what actually caused such pain. Izyk couldn't pinpoint the moment he decided to care about what bounced around in her beautiful mind, but he convinced himself it was only because distractions would set her back from creating a winning invention.

"Is Potek your bird?"

"No." Izyk chuckled. "He's just a companion. I found him when he was young and tossed him some bread. Ever since, he always thinks I have something to share."

"He's very unique."

Izyk rubbed at his stubbly chin. "He's the only bird I know of with such gifts. I've tried following him once to see if he had a hidden nest somewhere with others, but he seems to just wander the court with no home to go to."

Piora nodded, the fire reflecting in her dark eyes.

"Who taught you to play?"

Izyk almost choked on his drink, not expecting such a question.

"I taught myself."

"How about your parents?" The question came out uncertain, as if she was cautious of stepping too far.

"They were poor. Once I turned five, they abandoned me in the middle of the market. They lost themselves in the crowd. I screamed for them, but they never came back. I knew my way home, but I didn't return there. Even then, I knew that I was a burden and that they left me on purpose. So I lived from abandoned building to building, moving around enough so I wouldn't get caught. Once I learned to play any instrument I could get my hands on, I started busking for coins."

At some point during his story, she had turned around, her head resting on the cushion of the couch. It urged him on.

"I came here to celebrate a particularly successful day, getting drunk, and falling asleep right here." He tapped on the couch. "Ludwik said he saw me at the markets sometimes, and that he loved my playing. After that, I would come here daily, getting a drink that I couldn't afford, but wanting the company of a friend. Sooner or later, I divulged my situation to Ludwik, and he let me sleep in his spare room for a small fee. I'm grateful everyday to have him."

A tear blossomed from his eye, and before he could wipe it, Piora's soft, gentle hand reached up and swiped it away. Her touch lingered there for a moment, and he wanted to pull her close to him, but he held back, letting her lead.

"I don't—" she stammered, and he kept quiet, refusing to interrupt her again. "I don't know my father. My mother slept with some random man after accepting her role as minister. Apparently it was because she always wanted a child, but never wanted to be tied down to marriage, so she picked someone she would never interact with again, a traveler of some sort. It doesn't bother me, that I'll never know that other side of me, but—and I know it's not the same—I feel like I was always a responsibility my mother needed to fulfill. I understand that feeling of loneliness, and finding comfort in something that I'm good at."

"Your lightning."

"I have a home I go to each night, with a mother who I think cares, yet even *I* feel like a burden and failure. I found companionship in that workshop, a friend who I love dearly. She keeps me sane and confident in my decision to move forward, even with all the risk involved."

She said nothing more as she faced the fire again and sipped on her drink. He thought the conversation was over, and that she would leave without another word.

But then she opened her mouth, and said, "I'm happy you found him, Izyk, and I'm even happier that I found you, too."

Ten

Piora headed to the workshop with a sense of guilt that clung to her like an uncomfortable second skin. Izyk had been so open and vulnerable with her, in a way that made her want to touch him and comfort him, but she couldn't offer him the same. She had held back. It's not that she didn't trust Izyk, but she worried about his response if she told him the truth.

The workshop was full today, as expected with the Undertaking looming closer and closer, a buzzing energy in the room.

Roksana looked pleased with herself as she focused on her invention. From Piora's perspective, her invention seemed to be a small box, but Piora knew not to judge based on appearance. So much of what they created was about the inside, where their power flowed.

On the other side of the large room, another inventor tinkered with a small model. He kept it close to him so as not to let the others get a good view, but whatever it was, must have been large because the model was of a three story building.

Another worked on their sketches, but she knew that it consisted of reworking designs versus starting new ones, because she had seen them developing prototypes before.

Piora headed to Daria's station...only to find it empty. She placed her hand on her hips, but before she could stand there in confusion for too long, Roksana said, "She never showed up today."

Turning to Professor Silo, he nodded in confirmation.

That worried Piora. Daria would *never* miss time at the workshop. Even though she needed every second she could get to brainstorm ideas, bounce them off of Professor Silo, Piora couldn't concentrate while her friend could be somewhere in the middle of a breakdown. So Piora rushed back outside, where the wind pushed her from behind, and headed to the boarding house.

The boarding house was just barely on the outskirts of town, only a few blocks from where the market was held. Piora knew that many of those without powers lived in this area, sequestered away from those considered gifted. She never wandered through this part of town. Why would she when so much of her life was connected to where power thrummed? Even Ludwik's tavern was on the opposite side of town, as most of his patrons had powers.

For some reason, she expected it to be cold and gray, but everything in her sight disproved her expectations. There was so much life surrounding Piora. Kids freely ran the streets; older folks sat on old wooden chairs and talked to their neighbors; others watered their small flower beds. There was art hanging outside windows, and drawn across the cobbled streets. She even heard music playing from an open window further down the road.

Perhaps it had been a mistake to avoid a place of such bountiful community.

Piora smiled at everyone she passed, and even stopped to help repair a broken lamp post. As the light glowed onto people's faces, Piora promised herself she would be back often to ensure these lights worked, and if her powers were zapped away if she lost the Undertaking, then she would find someone else to take over. Once she made it to the boarding house, she had to push the old wooden door open with so much force that she was out of breath as she stepped inside.

The building was quiet, but she could hear voices echoing down the hall. She followed the sound, passing countless rooms, until she arrived in a backroom where various groups of people chatted and played games together.

Eyes turned towards her, watching her suspiciously. It was fair, she was a stranger to this place.

Yet, her eyes landed on the one person who was alone.

Daria lay on her stomach on the plush burgundy rug, colorful pieces of one of her favorite puzzles laying astray around her. A sign of stress, Piora had learned in their few months of friendship.

Piora got on her knees, a few feet away from the puzzle pieces, so as not to disturb her friend's thoughts.

Piora had once suggested that her friend get a new puzzle, but she refused to hear it, yelling at the top of her lungs. Apparently, her older brother had made it, painting a scene, cutting the hundred pieces into shapes, and sanding it down into perfection. It was one of the only items she had from her village. She had told Piora it had reminded her of exactly why she had left, and why each day she pushed to return as the winner of the Undertaking. This was a large town with resources and access to anything one needed only footsteps away, but the smaller villages weren't as privileged.

"Did something happen?" Piora asked cautiously.

Her friend didn't look up from where she was fitting together two pieces as she said, "No, this isn't a stress build, just a 'I need a break build.' My invention is coming together *too well*, and I think that's making me nervous." Her dark brown eyes then widened as if regretting her words. "Sorry, I know you're still struggling."

Piora shrugged. "I'm happy that you're having a better time than me."

"We still have two months. You will pull it together by then."

"Maybe...And maybe you'll win it all."

Piora thought that Daria deserved that—more than she did for sure. But the fact that she had Izyk depending on her too made her reconsider how much she wanted this. Then, she also remembered the latest news from her mother about losing her powers if she lost the Undertaking. It was a conundrum that grew with each passing day.

"I don't look at it as winning or losing. As long as we create something using our gifts, then we accomplished what we were set out to do. Winning puts too much pressure on something that I'm just lucky enough to do," Daria explained.

"You have a much better outlook on this than me."

"I don't put pressure on myself, or have anyone else to put it on me. In some ways, that makes me luckier than you."

"What would you do with the money?" Piora asked, even though she almost didn't want to know.

Daria craned her neck up, her lips pursed as she thought. "I think I would buy a home in town so I wouldn't need to sleep here, and so I could have my family visit whenever. Then, I would travel, to see what the rest of the courts needed. So many of the inventions we create are about bettering *our* lives, but the lives of those living in the other courts aren't considered. I want to change that. There would be hesitance at first, but I know, overtime, people would put their pride aside and accept them."

Daria had a glow about her when she spoke—nothing to do with the powers she beheld, but something that ran deeper. A positivity and desire for more. It reminded Piora so much of Izyk, and perhaps what drew Piora to him.

The Lightning Court didn't export many of their inventions, only a select few. Piora always found it odd, but apparently it would be difficult to sustain too many of their inventions without someone from this court fueling them with their power, and few volunteered to permanently station themselves away from their home court. Plus, the other courts had their own gifts that they relied on. It would be seen as an insult to act as if the Lightning Courts were required for them to live better, easier lives.

"I think that sounds wonderful," Piora said past a lump of pride in her throat that she struggled to swallow down.

"What do you plan on doing with the money?"

Piora dragged a puzzle piece around the floor with her finger. "I'm giving it away."

"Really?" Daria perked.

"Don't be so shocked. I'm a good person, too."

"Oh, it's not that I don't think that you're kind, but it just seems so counterintuitive to do in this court."

"What do you mean?"

Her friend sighed. "I mean that this court is all about caring for yourself, so much so that we don't look out for others. We view everyone as gifted or giftless, a divide most other courts don't have. People are grateful for those with powers because they fight to ensure that the whole court can live another year, but those without powers aren't shunned because they, too, provide for their respective courts in their own unique ways. Unfortunately, what happens here is just a product of our circumstances. Many don't think that what the giftless offer is enough." She shrugged, as if what she said didn't hold immense meaning, and then a dubious grin crossed Daria's face. "Unless you're only saying that you'll help so that the Gods will see that goodness and think your invention worthy."

"That's insulting. I would never."

"I know." Daria smiled. "Have you decided who exactly would be honored with the money?"

Piora pressed her lips together, but she could feel a blush rising to her neck and cheeks. "I promised half of it to someone, and the other half is to be determined." Though looking around her, she would like to help out the other giftless somehow. They could use the reminder that they offered something unique and special to the court, too.

"And who is this special someone," Daria teased.

Piora hesitated to disclose the person's identity. For the last week or so, Izyk had been privately hers. She didn't want to burst their little bubble. But...she also couldn't keep her mouth shut about him forever, and Daria was the safest person to reveal it to.

"A musician I met at one of my mother's services."

"That man must know how to use his fingers."

Piora's mouth gaped. "I never said it was a man!"

Her friend ignored her. "What does *he* plan to do with the money?"

"I don't know. He hasn't told me."

"Hopefully something honorable."

Piora pulled at her sweater to get some cool air. "He lives in a room on top of a tavern, so perhaps somewhere more permanent and comfortable to live."

"Instead of guessing, you could just ask him."

"I—" she clamped her mouth shut. "I'm not sure I want to know. It will make me feel even more guilty if I don't win."

"It also might give you the inspiration to keep going. Who knows, what he needs might be something worth making better."

Piora never thought of it that way. Perhaps Daria was right—knowing exactly what she was pushing to win for might help her get the gears inside her mind to turn right and click. The only question being: did he want to tell her? Izyk might have chosen to keep it private for a good reason, and she didn't want to overstep, especially when she had hidden so much of herself from him.

But maybe this was the perfect opportunity to be honest with him.

A secret for a secret.

Eleven

Their next meeting didn't take place for another week. Piora had showed up and told Izyk she needed a short break to focus on her Undertaking invention. Plus she wanted to spend more time with her friend, who she had been neglecting.

Izyk didn't mind. He used his time to lock himself in the chapel when there was no service, to sit in front of the piano and compose. But nothing felt right. The piece that would welcome the town to his music hall refused to form itself, but at least he had the courage to try again after so many months of avoiding it.

He wanted to find the right sound, a mixture of joy and ethe-realness, something moving that transfixed the audience and urged them to return.

It was a challenge he had been fighting for years, but with the possibility of the music hall becoming his, his time ran shorter and shorter.

The only person he allowed to disturb him was Ludwik, who would come in the afternoon with a hot meal. Ludwik knew that when Izyk got lost in his music, he would struggle to get himself back into the world.

Piora's mother would wander in and out as she prepared the altar, giving him a downcast glare, telling him she was not pleased with him. Did she know that he and her daughter had begun to grow closer? Did she know that Izyk wanted to kiss her again?

Did Piora even know how much she captivated him?

Her dedication and care was something he was honored to be a recipient of. Yet, deep down, he knew that once this was over, she would want to go their separate ways, when he would no longer be of use to her. So Izyk promised himself to make the most of the time they had so she could win this Undertaking, making both her mother and the Gods proud.

"Sorry I'm late," Piora said in a fluster as she stormed into the tavern. "I lost track of time."

Izyk checked his pocket watch, and she was only two minutes late—nothing to be so apologetic over.

"I hope you were at least getting lost in that beautiful mind of yours with ample ideas for the Undertaking."

Piora stopped, either surprised at the compliment or at how wrong he was.

"Something like that," she responded.

She seemed nervous, and not her usual state of anxiousness. Something was eating at her, and he was going to find out what.

"What's wrong?"

She got straight to the point. "What are you planning to use the money for? I've never asked for...reasons, but it might help motivate and inspire me."

Oh. He supposed he hadn't disclosed that information to her. Not intentionally, but he guessed a part of him was scared to admit it out loud. The music hall was personal to him. With what she was doing for him, she had the right to know, though.

"How about I show you?"

Piora bit her lip but nodded her head. Her hair was back in an updo, giving him a better view of her features. As much as he enjoyed the long locks she had, he liked seeing her face more; he admired the determination that shone in her dark eyes.

He grabbed his usual wool coat, the one he'd had for years. It luckily held up, though he had to resew the buttons too many times to count, and the pockets were susceptible to ripping. And of course, there was Potek, who changed the color almost daily. Today, it was sunset pink. Piora eyed it, but didn't question it further. He hoped the bird found him so he could change it to something more neutral. Otherwise, Izyk stood out too much amongst the other townspeople.

When Piora raised one of her brows, he told her, "It's a bit of a walk, so I'm glad you're dressed for the weather this time."

They hadn't spoken yet about what had sent her running through the streets, destroyed and disoriented, until she had reached him. He was giving her time, and while he had a feeling the truth would come out, he wasn't sure if it would strengthen their growing bond, or ruin it forever.

Piora had spent the last week second guessing everything. Was she making the right choice by participating in the Undertaking, especially with her powers on the line? Was letting her heart fall for the man that guided her towards her dreams the right call?

She didn't know, and that uncertainty began to eat away at her.

The only thing she had decided with confidence was that she wanted to tell Izyk the truth of her problems, even if it would crush him to know it.

She needed his objective ear, one away from her mother and the other Undertaking participants.

First, though, she wanted to see where he was taking her. A pride swelled in her chest knowing how much he cared about whatever it was. He was so excited that he was walking twice as fast as usual, and she had trouble keeping up.

"Slow down," she whined. "I'm shorter than you."

He turned around and finally realized how much further ahead he had gotten. "Sorry, Sparkling. I want to make it before it gets dark."

"This court is always dark and gray. That's why the electric lights are such a blessing."

"This place doesn't have any."

Where could he possibly be taking her that didn't have lights? Every building in the court had them.

"You're not taking me to the bottom of the sea, are you?"

He chuckled as she finally caught up to him. "We don't have an invention for that yet." He rubbed at his chin. "Maybe that could be it!"

"Be what?"

"Your invention. It could be a small enclosure enough to fit two or three people that sinks to the bottom of the ocean, so that we can learn what lurks there."

"Half of the population of the Rain Court could tell you that," Piora mumbled. When he rolled his eyes, Piora decided to entertain his idea, because she realized it couldn't hurt to consider every possibility. "And how exactly would it get back up?"

Izyk considered the question as they got to a part of town that was quieter and darker than the main streets. "Maybe someone who is not inside the machine has an object that controls it."

"That sounds complicated and not necessary. We have our own issues up here."

He flicked her cheek. "I think it would be *fascinating*."

She swatted him away. "And what if this device drifts too far, and becomes lost. I wouldn't want to be stuck in there until the air runs out."

Izyk shivered, as if thinking about that horrific notion. "Maybe you're right."

As usual, Piora didn't voice, but his sideward glance told her that he read her mind. He gently bumped his shoulder next to hers and laughed.

"You're too smart for me, Sparkling."

"Let's go." She ignored the compliment and the way it quickened her pulse.

Although the street lights barely sputtered an inch of light, Piora could still recognize the uniqueness of this part of town. The buildings all looked different, the architecture intentional. Definitely done by the hands of Thunder Court residents, capable of moving stone and rocks without breaking a sweat. Much different than the uniformity of the central part of the court. It all felt very…Izyk.

After another block of dead streets, one whose pavements had not been fixed for longer than acceptable—Piora had to be careful not to trip in the holes—they stopped at a large building. Piora squinted at it, memories of her childhood flashing before her.

"It's the old music hall," Izyk clarified. "It shut down ten years ago."

Even after all these years, the building still stood, proud and beautiful. The red brick contrasted with the grays and browns of the rest of the town, and the two talls spires that flanked the window with a design resembling a bird at the center gave it character that wasn't found in newer structures.

"It's magical," Piora whispered more to herself than Izyk, but he still heard her.

"It's even better on the inside."

"I vaguely remember."

"Let's bring those memories back," Izyk said as he stepped towards the door.

"What?"

"We're going inside, Sparkling."

Piora shook her head. "We can't. There's chains over the door. It's locked."

Izyk snorted and easily released the chains from the door and opened it. "I've been here too many times to count."

Piora hesitated, but Izyk had already stepped inside, so she had no option but to follow.

"I can't get in trouble. What will people say when the minister's daughter is caught trespassing? My mother will kill me before I even know what's happening."

"Relax." At Piora's unrelaxed face, he added, "We can go if you're truly uncomfortable."

She was uncomfortable and nervous, but she wanted to see what made Izyk so excited about this place.

She pushed him further inward. "Only for a short time."

His smile was so bright that she knew that whatever happened afterward, even if she ended up dead, would be worth the risk.

"Look up," he said.

She did.

The ornate, vaulted ceiling was beyond words. The hand painted designs between the cross sections of wooden beams were beyond comprehension—such talent and skill would be required to create illustrations so stunning.

"And we haven't even gotten to my favorite part."

They passed through one more set of doors, and across the next large room was a stage. Piora now remembered the sounds produced from this room when a full orchestra had played, how it had moved her so deeply, even at a young age.

"You want to buy this place?"

He nodded, as if too lost in his own emotions to speak. She let him take it in as she, herself, let the quiet energy of the music hall soothe her.

"If I—or anyone else—doesn't purchase it from the bank in the next few months, they will knock it down. This piece of history will be gone and forgotten."

"That's horrible," Piora said. Why would the town not want to preserve the history?

Izyk wiped at his eyes and headed to the stage, where a piano still occupied it. He sat down, put his hands on the keys, and played.

Piora had to sit down in one of the audience seats as soon as the notes hit her ears; the rawness of his internal state was so evident in the way he played. He had his eyes closed, letting his heart lead him. The outcome was mesmerizing.

"Come here," he said, when he stopped the first song. She rose from the seat and climbed the stairs to meet him. He scooted over, giving her room to sit next to him on the bench.

He gently took her hand and guided her through the song. He told her which fingers to use, which tempo to follow, and once she had somewhat gotten it, they played together. It was slow and not as pretty as when he had played it alone, but it felt right.

He looked down at her and smiled. Those golden brown eyes were damning. They would end her and begin her anew. How they held his determination and passion and bravery. How they called her to not be afraid of the unknown—and to try, even when the outcome was not certain. This man, who had been left alone as such a young boy, never let anything or anyone stop him from dreaming of his goals, even when others, no doubt, would scoff at the impossibility of it all.

Piora knew then that she had no more worries about telling him everything. She wanted to open her soul to him in the same way he was doing now. But first...she wanted to do something that would grant her the courage.

"I want you to cut my hair."

Twelve

"You're braver than you look, Sparkling," Izyk said as Piora used the sink to dampen her hair.

She hadn't spoken much since she'd made her request to him. When she uttered the words, Izyk had been rendered frozen. One would think that Queen Ludelle of the Snow Court was using her powers on him.

Yet, Piora hadn't backed down. She wanted to do this, and he wouldn't deny her. They went straight back to the tavern, and he retrieved the pair of scissors that he used to trim his beard on the occasions he grew it out.

Piora sat down at the stool Izyk brought up. Luckily, it was tall enough that she was at a comfortable height for him to do his work.

"Are you nervous?" he asked. He could feel the tension rolling off her in waves, but he thought she was making the perfect decision. That hair carried weight, and she needed to let it go.

She nodded, but then said, "I don't even remember what I look like with short hair."

"Well, I can fix that."

Piora stared at his hands and blushed. "The only reason I'm asking you to do it is because I trust those precise hands to not ruin my hair."

He gave her a wicked smile. "My hands are excellent."

She rolled her eyes, and he took in the sight of her so relaxed around him. He guessed there were only a few people she felt like she could be herself with, and he hoped he eased her enough to be one of them.

"How much are we cutting?" he asked as he opened and closed the scissors for extra effect.

"Let's start here." She used her hands to indicate to stop at just above her breasts. "Then, we can go shorter if I'm comfortable."

He saluted her and began. He pulled all her hair behind her so he could cut straight across evenly. He brushed his fingers through the smooth tresses, the brassy blonde glowing against the light above them. It was overwhelmingly soft, and smelled of amber and vanilla. Like comfort. Like home.

He didn't allow himself to get distracted by the rush of desire coursing through him. He started cutting, and she flinched at the first crisp sound of the scissors.

"No regrets," he said sternly. There would be no room for doubt here. He would only build her confidence up because she was the best thing to happen to him in a long time.

"No regrets," she repeated quietly to herself like a mantra.

He finished off cutting to where she wanted and brought the hair back over her shoulders.

"Take a look."

Piora turned towards the speckled mirror, and he swore a tear slipped from her eyes. He didn't comment, letting her decide how she felt about it. She touched her hair and moved it around.

"I want it shorter."

He only nodded, but inside, pride swelled.

"To my shoulders this time," she clarified, her back now straighter, as if no longer regretting her decision.

He sliced through the next layer of hair as his own confidence grew. He cut to the desired length, then turned the scissors vertically to add more depth to the ends so the line wasn't so stark.

It was quiet, the only sound was the snipping of the scissors and the rush of wind from a storm raging outside. A boom of thunder shook the old tavern. Izyk swore at Buraza, the Goddess of Thunder.

"It's done," he said, with a sigh of relief. He was impressed with his own work; he just hoped Piora would feel the same.

As Piora glanced at herself again, he could see the anxiety that rolled through her first before a quiet joy overtook her face, hints of glowing delight stained her cheek as they reddened just a smidge, and the gold in her eyes pulsed with light. It was as if, for the first time, she was looking at a version of herself that truly felt like her own. Her arms glittered with a jolt of power.

"It's going to be so much easier to manage," she finally said as she touched the ends of her hair that reached a little past her chin.

Of course she focused on the practicality of it instead of the significance of such an action.

"It's something that you chose for yourself without listening to anyone else's opinion, and have discovered that you're happy with it." He could tell that Piora let her mother sway her decisions. "You can stop doubting yourself now. Trust that you know what you want for yourself better than others."

They were staring at each other through the mirror, her back still to him as she was seated. His hands rested on her shoulders, and she lifted one of her hands and placed it over his. His heart halted and restarted, and a zap of desire coursed through him again. He knew it wasn't her magic that was responsible for it—just her.

Through the mirror, she met his gaze, then asked, "And what if I said I wanted you?"

He couldn't breathe, but his body knew before his mind that he wouldn't deny her what she asked because he wanted it, too. The other hand, the one not pinned under her heat, dragged up to her neck and back down the length of her arm.

"I'm all yours, Sparkling."

Thirteen

Every part of her body came alight at his touch. He moved his hands towards the hem of her thick sweater. He swept it over her head, and her exposed body chilled until his warm hands roamed over her back, trailing a feather light touch up her spine, to her shoulder, along the subtle golden lines marking her as one with the power of lightning.

Their eyes were still on each other in the mirror, and she watched his devastated face take her in.

"So, this is what you're hiding under there."

She blushed, dipping her head, wanting to hide herself now, but she groaned as he softly pinched both of her nipples. She leaned her head back against him, and even through his pants, she could feel his hardness pressing on her.

"Don't you dare cover yourself now," he said through gritted teeth, as if he were in pain, as if just seeing her body was enough to destroy him.

She wasn't certain why she wanted to bare herself physically before revealing all the truths she had been holding back, but it felt right. She was confident that he would take care of her, that he would understand the importance of this moment. And Piora's trust in Izyk was the greatest gift she could offer.

Her eyes were closed as he continued massaging her breasts, but she could sense his eyes on her, reveling in what he was able to do to her with such a simple touch. She wanted those hands in other places.

"Get up," he ordered, but not in a harsh way. She did. As he picked up the stool to move it aside, she had to fight the urge to brush her fingers through her newly cut hair. There was a fresh breeze against her neck that she hadn't felt before, and the wispy ends of her hair tickled her jaw. She didn't have a chance to linger on this new facet of herself.

When Izyk returned, he snared her chin and dipped his head slowly. Their lips were so close, yet not touching. They breathed into each other, and she allowed the moment to steady her.

"Are you sure this is what you want?"

The hesitance, his own unsureness, broke something in her. The man who was always confident in himself, and in the world, was growing doubtful in front of her.

She didn't let the concern fester as she rose up on her toes and pressed her lips to his. He didn't hold back as he led her towards the wall. She crashed into it, the paneling rattling.

She wanted to say that she hoped that Ludwik didn't hear or dare inspect the cause of the noise, but Izyk's lips were ravaging hers—she could barely breathe, much less vocalize her concern.

His soft lips and stubbled jaw created the perfect combination as his tongue slid in. She opened for him easily, and he groaned as she nipped his bottom lip. She grabbed his hips and pulled him closer, needing something, *anything*, to stabilize her. She felt dizzy and light all because of him.

"You're everything," he said as he pulled back, resting his forehead against hers. His breaths were heavy, as if he, too, was struggling to hold himself back.

The words hit her gut in a way that had her wanting to give everything to this man, and to never hold back again. Her hands roamed under his sweater, the muscles underneath flexing. Then she traveled lower, tracing over the hardness still captive in his pants. He hissed as she pressed upwards with the heel of her hand.

"Do you want these off?" he asked, his voice pained.

"Yes," she whispered back.

He grabbed her shoulders, then slowly dragged his fingers down to her hands, and held them.

With a swift motion, he lifted her arms up over her head and pressed them against the wall. She was restricted and at his mercy. He kissed her neck, and she arched towards him.

Against her throat, he said, "Only if I get to take yours off first."

"Please," she whined, and he chuckled against her skin.

He lifted her and carried her over to the bed. Gently laying her down, he stood there and watched her. She reached for the button on her pants, but he stopped her by climbing onto the bed, overtop her, trailing kisses on her clavicle, both her breasts, and her abdomen, until he got to the top of her pants. He unbuttoned and pulled them down, along with her underwear.

She shivered as all of her was bare to him.

"You're beautiful."

A tear slipped, and luckily he was too focused on her body to notice before she wiped it away. It wasn't from sadness, but such an overwhelming feeling of being worshiped by someone like him.

He licked her sensitive nub and pressed his tongue down on it. The sensation was so intense, her legs, on instinct, shut closed around his head.

"Relax," he said gently, as he rubbed at her outer thighs. "I want you to feel good, but tell me when it's too much."

She nodded, opening her legs back up. His tongue swirled around that bundle again, this time slower, but she didn't want it like that. She wanted him unleashed.

"You can go harder."

He listened to her without question, trusting that she knew her own limits. She couldn't hold back the moan, one so loud, she knew without a doubt that Ludwik and any unlucky patrons would know exactly what was going on in this room. Yet, she didn't care, because having Izyk like this would be worth the embarrassment.

Izyk then added his fingers, dipping them into her drenched core, curling the fingers upwards to rub at the most sensitive spot. He knew exactly what he was doing, and perhaps the Piora of days ago would consider that dangerous, but after today, all she could feel is bliss, and joy, and freedom.

He understood her.

It wasn't scary. It was beautiful.

She was the most beautiful thing he'd ever seen. The sounds that escaped her lips were setting him ablaze, but it was the softness of her skin that drove him close to madness.

He pumped his fingers slowly, getting her adjusted to the sensation, but he could tell she wanted more. He was beginning to lose his own control.

"Please," she kept saying. And who was he to deny her of what she so clearly craved?

He backed away and took off his own sweater and pants, his erect cock bulging at the tip.

She was anchored on her elbows, her newly short hair framing her face perfectly—no longer was her hair a shield, a way to hide herself from him. He could see all of her and soak in the affects of her pleasure.

She swallowed. "It's so big."

He pumped his length, once, twice, and her eyes glazed over. "I'll go slow."

She nodded, but added, "Don't be gentle with me though. I'm not porcelain."

He was on top of her again, his cock right near her entrance. "Never," he whispered into her ear. "Put me inside you."

Taking his cock in her hand, he hissed as she guided him inside. She whimpered when he sunk halfway in, so he stayed still for a moment. She breathed deeply as she slowly pushed him further and further, until he was fully seated inside her.

The entire time he pressed kisses on her, reminding her that she set the pace, that she was in control.

He rubbed her clit, bringing her pleasure past the burn. "Tell me when you're ready."

Her eyes were closed, but at his words, she opened them. He could have sworn the golden lines on her body sparked like lightning for him, her powers clawing their way out to meet him.

"I'm ready."

Izyk slowly pulled back out and in, thrusting at a pace that he knew would make her feel good and overwhelmed.

She practically squealed, biting his shoulder.

"Don't hold back," he muttered against her skin. "I want you unleashed for me."

She cried out at his words, and he knew then that he could go harder. He drove fast and deep, getting at the farthest spot that would make her see the Gods themselves.

She was holding onto him, her hands clawing his back, and he liked how she used him as her anchor. As they moved, the floorboards and bed creaked, and he knew that Ludwik would give him a mouthful over the noise tomorrow—but he didn't care about anything except the woman beneath him.

When he thought that she was close, she said the unexpected. "I want the mirror next to us so I can watch."

He growled at the suggestion. "Your mind is genius, Sparkling."

She snorted. "Just do what I ask."

He did, almost tripping over himself in excitement. When he was back inside her, they both turned to watch themselves. His cock slid perfectly into her wetness, and her mouth circled open with a moan.

"We're so beautiful," she said past deep breaths.

He could feel her beginning to tighten around him. "It's because we're perfect together," he said. Words that were a gamble because although he felt that way, he didn't know where she stood.

But it took her over the edge. She arched and twitched beneath him, and he worked her through one orgasm directly into another as he relentlessly rubbed her clit.

He was close, himself, and he took her breast in one of his hands and squeezed.

"Fuck," he swore, losing himself in colliding waves of Piora and pleasure. "Fuck..."

"Let go," she said, bringing his mouth to hers. This time, the kiss was sloppy and wild. Their tongues tangled together, as they fought for dominance. Within moments, he pulled out, his seed erupting onto her stomach and breasts.

He could barely breathe when she dragged her fingers through it and licked it off.

Izyk knew then that no one would ever come close; her body and soul were made for him.

Fourteen

Piora had fallen asleep at some point and had woken up with a realization, like a blow in the gut—her mother must be worried sick over her whereabouts. But it didn't stir her into action. It was too late at night to go anywhere, and the man who had both wrecked and reformed her was holding her tight. Sheets covered their nude bodies, and she could still feel the strength of him against her, his arms wrapped around her waist like a security blanket. She savored the way it calmed her, the way she copied his slow breathing to relax her heart.

She could deal with her mother in the morning.

Now, she wanted to exist in this sacred shell and be with this man without worrying about anything that needed to be done outside this room.

Sensing her alertness, Izyk's eyes fluttered open. The golden brown, usually so bright that glowed, was dim, as if it too were relaxed and content.

He immediately shifted to his back, pulling her on top of him. She rested her arms and chin on his broad chest, tangling her legs with his.

As he ran his fingers through her short hair, he asked. "Do you regret it?"

Piora knew he wasn't asking about her hair. "No," she said confidently.

"Good."

She traced her fingers along his skin, creating swirls and whirls, as if she could imprint the same golden lines she had onto him. "I have something I need to tell you, though." She tried keeping her tone light, indicating that it wasn't serious, but Izyk still stiffened beneath her.

"What's wrong?"

Piora wished she had a drink to get through this, but she wouldn't cower away from telling him the truth—not when he had been so open and vulnerable with her.

"Do you remember that day when I ended up at your door in tears?" He nodded from beneath, but gave her the space to continue. "My mother had just revealed something to me that completely changed everything. She—" Piora struggled to get the words out. She concentrated on Izyk's hands on hers. "She told me that if I compete in the Undertaking, then I will lose my Sight, and if I compete and lose, I will lose both of my powers. I would become giftless." She hated that word on her tongue.

Izyk's hands stopped moving, and she could feel the tension and confusion rolling off of him.

"You have the Sight? Like minister Kaplana?" he asked harshly.

"I do."

"And you have the power of lightning in your veins."

She only nodded this time, acknowledging his words. She could tell he was processing it all, the fact that she had two forms of powers while he had none. Although deep down she knew it was something that was entirely out of her control, guilt clawed at her insides.

"Having the gift of Sight is considered the greatest honor from the Gods. One I would think you would accept."

Piora sighed, her eyes beginning to burn. "I've never wanted to become the minister of this court. I have dreamed of participating in the Undertaking since I was a child, since I knew I had lightning, too. My dreams have always felt foreign and wrong, but my lightning has always been an extension of me."

"And you're willing to risk them both over what exactly? To prove a point?"

Piora flinched as she rolled off him. She stood up, gathering the sheet to cover herself. Izyk lay there bare, not attempting to move.

"I'm willing to risk it because I find the inventions we can create to be meaningful. I'm willing," she said with force, "to risk it for you—so that I can give you the money to buy the music hall!"

"You shouldn't," he responded, his voice strained. "I'm not worth it. You should accept your gift of Sight and be grateful to have any gifts at all."

"That's the most foolish thing I've ever heard you say. I don't need to just accept everything that I am given."

"You don't want to be giftless, Piora!"

She stumbled back, shocked at his outburst, but even more so at the use of her name. He never did; she was always Sparkling to him.

"Being giftless is a curse. Everyone looks down upon you."

"That's not true..." Yet, she was brought back to that boarding house, where the giftless were outcasted.

He finally stood up and reached her. Without a word, he turned around.

Piora gasped at what covered his skin, the dark lines of black that resembled lightning, the opposite of her own golden ones. She reached out her hand, pressing gently; the lines slightly raised as if they were scars, cursed with darkness like a disease.

"How?" she barely breathed out.

"When they discover you are giftless, they mark your skin in a place where few see, where I rarely see, but in those moments where I do catch a glimpse of everything I do not have, I am reminded of how useless I am. It's a way to mock us, to remind us we do not have the mark of lightning."

Her hand shook, unable to process how someone could do something so vile to innocent people. Who thought they had the right?

Piora had an inkling of the answer, but she still had to know. "And who brands your skin like this?"

His voice shuttered as he said the words. "The minister."

A ringing echoed in Piora's ears. She moved to sit down on the bed again, the sheets long forgotten.

Izyk kneeled before her, holding both of her thighs, his calloused fingers rubbing against her, as her mind swirled with so many all-consuming thoughts. Her mother had unforgivably hurt Izyk, along with many others who did not deserve such pain.

"Was it the Gods who asked for it to be done?"

Her faith in them had been so strong, but...perhaps she was placing her trust in the wrong people. And a part of her needed to know that it wasn't her mother's decision.

"I don't know. I would assume so."

"I'm sorry," she apologized, hiding her face in her hands. She bent forward, and he pressed a kiss to her head. "I should be comforting you."

He brought her in for a hug as she fell to her knees with him. "Don't apologize for something you have no control over."

How could he be so gentle with her? How could he have spent so much time with the daughter of the woman who had marred him? It was a strength, Piora realized, one not many had. Not everyone could face what he had and come out the other side still fighting. He was a soul bred from his own love and passion, yet she could see he needed that part of him tended to sometimes. Piora promised herself then that she would, everyday if needed.

She pulled back and looked at him, wiping away her tears. "You're worth it."

"What?"

"You're worth the risk, Izyk. You're worth my every second, and the potential of becoming giftless." He opened his mouth to protest, but she placed a finger over his lips to shush him. "Being giftless doesn't make you worthless. Look at the beauty you're able to create with just your hands. The sounds of joy and sadness. *That* is a gift in its own right. You need to believe that."

"I don't want you to go through what I did."

She shook her head, refusing to stand down. "It's my choice. I want to do this. For you, for others, and for myself. If I lose, then at least I know I tried by following my heart."

"Now you're sounding like me."

"Because you inspire me, Izyk."

And in that moment, Piora now knew what she would invent. Something that would hold his beauty.

"And you're my destiny, Piora."

She kissed him deeply, lingering in his touch and taste because once they stepped out of this room, the reality of what they discussed would crash on them like the booms of thunder.

Fifteen

A renewed energy sparked through Izyk, his footsteps lighter and his posture tall. All because of her.

Piora had ripped him apart and bound him back together. He thought he would be left angry after she revealed how she held two powers, but once he let go of his own insecurities—thanks to her—he ended up understanding her frustration with it. The pressure that weighed on her would be debilitating, and he couldn't blame her for refusing to accept the gift of Sight. Being a minister required a blind faith in the Gods, and he knew Piora's was now cracked with what he told her, what he showed on his back.

He rested at the tavern after a long day of busking, his hands frozen from being outside so long. He still believed that Piora would win the Undertaking, but Izyk didn't know if he would be able to accept the money. He didn't want her doubting for a second that what they had was only about that.

"You're thinking," Ludwik said as he wiped up some spilled ale.

"Contrary to what you believe, I do have a working mind in here," Izyk tapped at his freshly shaven head. The strands had been growing too long for his liking. After spending so much time from one abandoned building to the next with an array of bugs as companions, he never let his hair grow out.

Ludwik rolled his eyes, but didn't push it. "I'm surprised I haven't had the honor of hearing you and Piora fuck it out again."

Izyk gave his friend a vulgar gesture. "She's busy."

It had been a week since that night, and Piora had locked herself away in the workshop. She visited him one time to inform him that she needed to focus on the Undertaking and that she hoped he wouldn't be upset. He kissed her deeply, hoping that she wouldn't forget him when she had the glory and fame of being this year's Undertaking winner.

"You've been busy, yourself. I barely see you, and when I do, you just head straight to your room to sleep."

Izyk chewed his lip. Ludwik had a point. Spending so much time with Piora, Izyk had been neglecting his longest friend, which was unacceptable.

"How's your nephew?"

Ludwik smiled. "He and his mother are traveling. He says the Solar Continent is beautiful."

The Solar Continent was situated across the sea just east of the Weather Continent. It was made up of four courts: Dawn, Day, Twilight, and Night.

"And how are the Undertakings there?"

"Just as intense. We really are lucky in this court that our lives aren't in danger."

Izyk shook his head, taking a sip of his drink and letting the alcohol coat his throat. "I never understood it. How the Gods decided it to be this way, why some courts have to face death and danger, while we just worry about the inventors creating something the Gods deem worthy." Though he supposed he now knew there was a risk involved in competing. Did everyone who lost have their powers taken, too? It brought his thoughts to his mother, who he learned years later had competed and lost. Was it shame that forced his parents to abandon him?

Ludwik sipped on his own drink. "Why should we question the will of the Gods?"

As if the Gods themselves had heard, a storm raged through, and the door to the tavern shot open.

A petite figure with bright blonde hair entered the tavern, her steps even and refined, even if her face told a different story. An angry energy brewed inside her, and Izyk knew she was about to erupt.

On him.

She stayed quiet and delicately sat on the stool next to Izyk. She didn't order anything, but both his and Ludwik's eyes were locked on the woman, readying for her to speak.

The minister of the Lightning Court, Piora's mother, wiped at the folds of her robes, straightening them out before she met Izyk's gaze.

"Are you the one who defiled my daughter?" Kaplana's displeased tone delighted Izyk because the woman deserved to be uncomfortable after the way she treated her daughter.

Izyk also knew that she wasn't asking about the sex, but about Piora's hair—especially after Piora told him the woman had no problem sleeping around to produce a child.

Smiling brightly, Izyk responded to the accusation. "She looks beautiful, doesn't she? I think it suits her."

"She is not meant to cut her hair if she is to be minister."

Ludwik and Izyk exchanged glances, knowing this would turn for the worse, but Izyk continued. "She doesn't want to be minister."

Kaplana seethed, her hands growing tense on her lap. "My daughter does not know what she wants."

"She wanted to cut her hair."

"And I suppose you were the one to fill her mind with such ideas?"

Izyk swallowed down a large gulp of his drink, making her wait longer for him to answer. "I did no such thing. She asked of her own free will, since she is her own person, who can make her own choices."

"I heard that she plans to give you the money if she wins."

The change in direction of the conversation unnerved him, but only for a second before he recovered. He should expect nothing less from a woman who had direct access to the Gods. A pop of wood cracked in the fire nearby. "Something she agreed to."

"Did she tell you what happens if she loses?"

Izyk hated where this was going. "She did."

"And yet you still are allowing her to continue with this, even if she might lose everything. I thought you cared about her."

He did, more than he ever imagined he would. And he knew the best way of showing his care and adoration for her was by giving her the opportunity to be free to follow her heart.

"Someone who is giftless is not someone who is empty. We are just as important as those with powers." Words he could only voice because of what Piora told him. He realized because of her that even the giftless had contributions to offer the court.

The minister snorted. "The Gods cursed you with nothing."

"Or they blessed us with a chance to find power in something else."

"Like your little music?"

Ludwik stepped in before Izyk could pounce on the woman. "Is there something you need? If not, I must ask you to leave. You are disrupting my business and other patrons."

Izyk hadn't realized how others were now looking at them.

"I was just leaving," she said.

She left a coin on the bar, even though she didn't buy anything. Even if Izyk could use every coin that he could, he pushed the metal over to his friend, refusing to accept anything from that woman. The only thing good about her was her daughter.

Sixteen

"Faster," Piora urged him from ahead. She was practically skipping down the cobbled streets, easily weaving through anyone in her way.

He didn't know the reason behind her excitement. One minute Izyk was in his room, the next Piora had burst in wild-eyed and determined to get him up from his bed. It had been almost three weeks without her presence, and he debated pulling her down to the mattress with him and ravaging her, but he had never seen her like this. His own curiosity won out. Minutes later, he was following her.

But after the initial surprise of her visit wore off, he was left with an uncertain dread coating his stomach. Kaplana's disturbance from weeks ago still rattled him. Perhaps he should be discouraging Piora from competing. Perhaps he was being selfish by keeping his mouth shut. They had made their deal before Piora learned of the possibility of losing her powers, but a part of him still believed she was only participating because she wanted to win him the money.

Piora leaned against an unlit lamp post. It was one of those rare days where the sun was above them, the rays glowing against Piora's beautiful hair. Since cutting it for her, she kept it down, and he always itched to reach out and run his fingers though the strands. He could tell a weight had been unburdened from her, that she felt freer now.

"Why are you so glum?" she asked, her concern evident.

"Sometimes even I need a day to be a broody bastard," he joked, trying to lighten the mood.

She narrowed her eyes at him, but didn't push it. He sighed internally.

"So, where are you taking me?"

"Don't you recognize the path?" she responded as they made a right turn, and as the buildings turned older and more worn down, he nodded to himself.

"The music hall."

She paused, as she worried her bottom lip between her teeth. "You don't mind, do you?"

The question, the nervousness, made her irresistible. He stepped forward, and they were so close. She craned her neck up. He couldn't stop himself as he brushed his fingers through her short hair, and as her eyes fluttered closed, he bent down to kiss her. She gasped into his mouth. As he swiped his tongue across her lips, she opened for him. She wrapped her arms around his neck, and he hoisted her up and pressed her against a nearby wall, uncaring if anyone saw them.

He trailed his mouth down her neck, pulling her sweater away and biting softly at the sensitive flesh. The way she moaned caused his hardness to edge on the side of pain. He wanted to dive into her core, to relieve his growing desire. But she seemed to have something else in mind, as she brought a hand down between them and began rubbing him through his trousers.

He panted, the sensation so intense that he knew he wouldn't last long.

"I want to touch your skin," she murmured against his neck.

He gritted his teeth as he leaned away slightly, and it provided her enough space to wedge her hand down into his pants and pull him out. His eyes widened at the action, but a determined smile was her only response. He anchored his hands against the wall, her head at the center, and he watched her mischievous smile widen as a garbled mess of swears escaped his lips while she stroked him. The friction was so intense as she neared his tip and squeezed. Then, before he could prepare, she sent small shocks of lightning onto him. At first, the zaps were unbearable, but as she moved at a steady pace, he began to feel the pleasure rock through his entire body. He was a heaving mess with each movement, and it didn't take long until he erupted into her hand.

As she pulled away, she displayed her wet hand, covered in his essence. "I see you missed me."

He didn't give her the satisfaction of a laugh as he sucked his own release from one of her fingers then the next. His eyes narrowed in on her the whole time.

"What was that for, anyway?"

She snorted. "An early thank you."

"For what?"

She shrugged. "You'll soon see."

He couldn't believe the woman he had in his arms. When he met her she was uptight and nervous, but he could see her budding confidence grow each day. It was never meant to happen, but he was falling for her, and he had nothing to hold onto for the slow descent.

"You're my devotion," he said.

He could feel her breath stop for a moment, and start again.

"You are my devastation," she replied, as she kissed him deeply.

He only hoped her words weren't a bad omen.

Izyk's presence wrecked her each time. As soon as they were alone together, she wanted him as close as possible. She wanted to worship him and be worshiped by him in return. There was such an even give and take between them. She never felt like she had to give up a part of herself when around him. She could just *be*. And that made her even more excited—but also absolutely terrified—to show him what she had created.

They snuck inside the music hall, though the whole area was, as usual, abandoned. Not a single soul was around to condemn them for their earlier actions. It had been thrilling and unplanned; Izyk inspired her to take chances in ways she would have shied away from before.

Piora led Izyk to the main performance area, up to the stage, and seated him at the piano bench. His first instinct was to place his fingers against the ivory keys. He played a short melody that weaved around them, as if it were Potek, flying around.

When he finished, his eyes were cleared, brighter.

"I didn't ask the first time, but how did this piano not get removed when they shut it down?" She would have assumed the bank would have sold it to the highest bidder.

Izyk rubbed his hand against the wooden instrument, savoring its beauty. A deep silence swallowed him, and she readied herself to let the subject go, but he finally spoke up.

"I bought it."

It must have been expensive. Most surely, it set him back far from his goal of buying the music hall.

"Do you regret it?"

He shook his head. "The day after my parents left me alone in that market, after they realized I had no power pumping in my veins, I came here. Well..." He snorted. "I snuck in. I didn't have money for a ticket, so I found the back door and ran inside before I was caught. It was a packed house that night, and I listened from behind a pile of boxes. When they caught me, the composer stopped them from throwing me out. He brought me next to him in the wings, so I could both listen and see the performance. I was captivated."

Piora took in each word, the nostalgia of the memory, the sadness of his haunting past, and the joyful discovery of his true love of music. Each facet of emotion shone on his face.

"After the show, the composer sat me at the piano and showed me how it was done. How to use my fingers to create a cacophony of sounds that could elicit whatever emotion I dared. It was him that motivated me to learn more. I could never open this music hall without this piano at its center."

"That's a lovely story," Piora could only say as she sat down next to him and rested her head on his shoulder.

"I thought the piano would be my salvation. I thought it held magic. I thought I would sit down after I bought the damned thing, and it would give me enough inspiration to write the masterpiece I need." He looked at her. "If you haven't guessed by our deal, it hasn't worked out that way."

"You'll find what you're looking for," Piora responded sincerely.

"What if I never create music again?"

She brought his hand over on top of her chest so he could feel her heart thrumming beneath. "I always have music, because you created music within me."

She let go, and his hand trailed upward to her neck, and further, to her cheeks. He stared into her eyes, and she smiled at him. She pressed a kiss to his fingertips as they brushed her lips. He pulled away, but he seemed to believe her.

Izyk cleared his throat as he scratched at his chin. His vulnerability pushed aside to reveal the cocky man beneath. "So, Sparkling, why are we here? Are we going to put on our own performance to christen it?"

She bumped her shoulder against his. "Disgusting."

"Worth a shot." He shrugged. "What we did outside only took off the edge of my desire for you."

"I have a gift," she laughed, as she ran backstage to acquire it. She returned with the object held behind her back.

She sat back down on the bench and placed the object on the piano in front of him.

He cocked his head to the right. "What is it?"

She didn't answer him. Only pressed one of the few buttons on the device. "Will you play for me?"

Izyk hesitated, but, within seconds, his hands were flying across the piano. Like always, he got lost in the music while Piora got lost in him.

When he played the final note, Piora pressed the button on the device again. Piora breathed deeply. This is when everything she had been working on in the past few weeks would be revealed. What if he hated it?

"I know..." She stumbled over her words. "I know you have a negative view of the inventions we make, but...but I'm hoping this one will be different."

Before she could overthink it, she pressed a different button on her invention, and the last few minutes of sound repeated itself back to them. Her questioning him to play, his music echoing across the hall. It all came back to them like a memory never lost.

Izyk's face remained stoic, and her heartbeat raced within her chest, picking up speed with each second of doubt. She was an idiot. Of course he hated it. He valued the power of a performance and this took that away and—

"So everyone can always have music." His voice was a whisper, but the large room allowed her to hear each syllable.

She nodded. "Everyone deserves to hear your magic."

When she was working on the design, she ensured exactly three recordings could be saved. As soon as the idea sparked, she knew she wanted his music to take the first spot. It would be what she played at the Undertaking.

"You're magnificent," he said. A tear fell from her eye, one she meant to wipe away, but Izyk got to it before her. "You are magnificent," he repeated, and punctuated it with a kiss so deep she became dizzy.

Izyk stood up and took her hand. His reverence for her turned to longing touches, turned to deep desire, as he removed all her clothes and showed her how much he loved her invention. The sounds of their adoration echoed loudly, their love making worthy of being imprinted into the device one day, once the music hall was officially purchased. As they each finished, the truth of their love glittered around them. No matter what happened beyond these walls, their faith was in each other, and Piora realized she could live the rest of her life with that being enough.

Seventeen

Piora glowed as she walked the streets back home. Izyk had taken his time learning every inch of her flesh, leaving her a writhing mess beneath him. She would never have enough of him, and after this Undertaking was over, and the music hall was his, they would talk about their future. Because this deal couldn't be the end of them. Piora couldn't continue on without him.

As she neared her house, Piora imagined a life with Izyk. She now knew what she would do with the portion of the money when she won: she would buy someplace to live, a home. Izyk could join her, so he would no longer live in a small room on top of the tavern. It would become a sanctuary for the both of them.

Her excitement grew enough that her lightning crackled up from her hands over her forearms. She smiled down at it.

When she entered the house, darkness cloaked her. She turned on the light, but the quiet told her of her mother's absence. Perhaps she had gotten stuck at the chapel for some reason. As the Undertaking neared, her mother always required more time with the Gods. Her dreams became more intense as they guided her.

Piora approached the kitchen, ready to make something to eat, when she stumbled upon the note on the table.

I need your assistance. Meet me at the chapel whenever you can.

Love,

The Gods' dutiful servant, Minister Kaplana

Piora shook her head at the signature. For once in her life, couldn't the woman just be her mother and not the minister?

She supposed her plans to take a bath and steep in the hot water long enough to prune would have to be delayed.

Back outside, it had begun to rain, a light drizzle that clouded the falling night into an eeriness Piora loved. The lights guided her onward, but it felt like everyone had sheltered for the evening.

Thankfully the chapel was not far. Her mother had made sure of it when she bought their house. She refused to have a long trek each day, and Piora couldn't blame her for that.

Before she entered, Piora looked up at the building, at the mosaic of colorful broken glass fused together to create a masterpiece. The window was crafted by the hands of this court, and Piora would never stop being in awe of what one could make with a vision and their time.

The first thing she noticed when she walked in was the silence. It felt odd for some reason, like the space should be filled with the sound of notes and chords. She gave the piano one glance, thinking about how Izyk had lifted her on top of the one in the music hall and feasted on her. Her face heated at the memory, but she took the stairs down to find her mother who, no doubt, was in the small prayer room in the basement of the chapel.

Downstairs, a bright light blasted at Piora's sensitive eyes. She blinked furiously, adjusting her sight before finally getting a glimpse of what stood before her.

There was a large spotlight on the ceiling beaming down against a lone chair. The kneeler had been pushed to the side, the portrait of Elektra gone. There were candles lit by the wall. The smell stood out to Piora. It was the usual scent of incense with some notes of something extra—but Piora hadn't noticed the shackles on the chair until it was too late.

"I'm so sorry, my child," the muffled whisper of her mother came from behind Piora. "This is for the best."

A blast hit the back of Piora's knees, and she fell forward, slamming down onto the stone ground. She tried using the chair in front of her as leverage to get back up, but her mother grabbed her legs and pulled her away.

"What are you doing?" Piora seethed through her fog-muddled brain.

When she finally got a look at her mother, her nose and mouth were covered with a cloth. That was when it hit her. There was something in the incense her mother burned that was causing the world to grow hazy.

Piora tried to stay alert, to not let whatever was now in her system overtake her senses, but with each shallow breath, she grew more tired.

"Don't fight it," her mother warned.

Piora attempted to kick her mother, but it was fruitless. Her energy had waned, and she could feel her body giving in.

"I hate you," she spat at her mother, but the words came out garbled and indecipherable. The last thing she saw before her eyes shut was her mother shaking her head down at her.

The first thing Piora noticed when her eyes opened again was the door to the prayer room. She could barely remember how and why she was here. How long she had been out was a mystery. She made to get up, but was restricted by the shackles at her wrist and ankles. She pulled at them, yanking hard. The action did nothing but rub her skin against the leather. It didn't discourage her from trying again, and again, and again.

"Come on!" she yelled through gritted teeth. As the memories resurfaced, Piora knew with confidence that whatever her mother had planned would change her drastically.

"I told you to not fight it."

Piora was breathing heavily, her hair sticking against her sweaty brow.

"Let me go!"

"I can't do that," her mother said casually as she seemed to be working on something, but Piora couldn't see from her vantage point.

Finally, her mother turned around—she looked feral with rage; her pupils were dilated and her usually perfectly combed hair stuck out from all angles.

"I am giving you a choice."

Piora's heart leaped at the words, because her mother's face told her she wouldn't like the options.

"One..." her mother circled her, but Piora refused to give in to the fear the minister was trying to stoke. "You don't compete and you become the minister, as is your destiny. Or two, you foolishly follow your stupid dream and lose it all."

"I'm not giving up," Piora stressed her words as she shook the chair. She would get out of this, and she would present her new invention. Damn her mother and damn the Gods for doubting her.

"Piora." The tone was condescending, like she was speaking down at a child. "You forget that the Gods tell me everything."

"I don't care what they say."

"You don't even have an invention to compete with." Her mother seemed to register the confusion on Piora's face. "You don't think I have an eye on that workshop? I'm told the progress of everything."

"Clearly not," Piora rolled her eyes. The device in her pocket was her lifeline. The fact the Gods hadn't passed along the information to her mother showed they liked watching how this would all play out. Piora and her mother were just entertainment for them, but Piora would use all her advantages to get out of here.

"What's that?" her mother snarled.

"Clearly you don't know it all," Piora said. "I've created something I am proud of. Something I think can win."

"There's still two weeks until the Undertaking. You had nothing last week."

Piora made another attempt at getting out of the chair, and this time she, along with the chair, toppled over. It didn't break the wood, and she was still stuck—yet she could hear the click she had been hoping for.

"You're only going to make what I do more uncomfortable," her mother tsked.

"You're not touching me."

"What I'm going to do with you if you don't agree to my terms will not require me to touch you."

"I'm not agreeing to anything," Piora whined from her awkward spot on the ground.

"But you don't even know my terms."

Piora remained straight-faced. She needed to get out of this, but she desperately wanted her mother to reveal whatever grand plans she had concocted.

"Do you want to hear?" Her mother crouched down, her long light hair swept at the ground, her ivory robes fanned around her. She smiled down at Piora. "You don't compete, you become the minister once I step down, and you are allowed to access my bank account and to do whatever you want with the money in the meantime. Then, once you become minister, your own account will be opened, and you'll watch it grow each year."

Piora swallowed. "What money?"

"The Undertaking entrance fee."

"I thought that was given back to the community to be able to produce the winning invention."

"Some." Her mother shrugged. "I keep a hefty sum."

"And the Gods allow it?"

"The Gods are slippery."

"And if I don't agree?"

Her mother's face hardened. "Do you know that every year there is a consequence to losing?"

Piora stiffened. "No."

"You, like many others, believe our Undertaking is a blessing in comparison to other courts, that the Gods favor us. In some ways, it's true. The Gods view our court as the pumping blood of the other courts because we invent objects that keep the courts running, even something as simple as a lightbulb has changed the trajectory of this whole continent. They need us to create an illusion. What would the Weather Gods be without us? They would have no one to control."

"What does that have to do with consequences?"

"This court's consequences are more subtle. Participants lose what they most desire if their invention is not chosen."

Piora blinked, letting the words sink in. "For me, it would be my power."

"Correct." Her mother nodded, but she wasn't distraught by it at all. She didn't care that Piora would lose what she wanted most. "Therefore, since I know you will lose if you walk into that room, why not get ahead of your fate?"

Piora's heart stammered in her chest. "Wh–what do you mean?"

"It means, if I get rid of your power now, maybe it will finally stop you from participating so you don't lose your Sight either."

"And this is all for some extra money?"

"This is for the best."

"I'm still competing." Because as much as her mother wanted to convince Piora she knew the outcome of the Undertaking, Piora was under the impression it was a bluff.

"Then, you leave me no choice."

One second Piora was on the ground, the next she was being heaved back up, and her skin sliced by a small blade. Blood welled at the palm of her hands, but she watched as her mother took the topaz Heart of the Lightning Court and smeared the crimson liquid over it. It was like the Heart was thirsty, as it swallowed her blood within itself.

"This will hurt," her mother warned.

Then, her lightning began to sizzle at her fingertips up along her arms towards her chest. Usually, her power never hurt her, but this time an excruciating pain pricked at her skin as her lightning fought her, as it was being leeched from her with every second the Heart feasted on her blood.

On the other side of town, Izyk was transported to someplace deep in his mind where no thoughts of self-doubt inflicted him. It was just his body and whatever part of his mind stored the music of his soul.

Piora had altered something within him. She had released him from the trap of the unknown and opened a destiny for him. With each stroke against the piano keys, the door opened wider and wider.

The song was a story. It had ups and downs, the notes deep and dark, then high and light. There were flashes of unexpected surprises, and as the song reached its climax, a crescendo boomed up, and up, and up. The height of the song was like standing on that cliff with Piora as she reached her hand out to the lightning that beckoned her. It was watching her being consumed by her passion for creation. It was the moans and breaths as he rocked in and out of her until she was a trembling form beneath him, until he kissed her skin back down from such deep pleasure.

He poured everything into the tune. And as he played the final note, a stillness washed over him. He no longer had to fear the future as long as Piora was in it. Even if he was never was able to buy this music hall, she would bring music to his life everyday. She was the rhythm he had been longing for his whole life, and together they created a beautiful beat. Everything else beyond her was extra.

He couldn't wait to tell her how much she meant to him. He couldn't wait to watch her win the Undertaking, and continue to cherish her powers for the beauty they could bring. He couldn't wait for her listen to the piece that would forever be dedicated to her.

Eighteen

The eve before the Undertaking had crept upon the court like a sly mouse. Izyk had not seen Piora since she had shown him her invention, but she had left a note for him with Ludwik. In it, she wrote how the stress and pressure were eating at her, and how she wanted time to perfect the invention. He had crumpled up the note, considered ignoring it, and took two steps towards the door before Ludwik called for him to stop. Apparently, Piora had looked worse for wear when she had stopped by, and perhaps, it would be wise to heed her plea.

So Izyk waited as long as he could. But with the Undertaking tomorrow, he wanted to tell her how she had inspired his song. He wanted to remind her of how special she was, and that no matter what happened tomorrow, he would forever be grateful for her. She was his muse, and he couldn't live life without her.

He would get her to come out of her house to talk to him so he could tell her he loved her. He loved her spark, her passion, her otherworldliness. He didn't care that she wielded not one, but two sets of powers, and was risking them both by competing. He didn't care how, for the rest of their lives together, he would be the ungifted lover by her side each day because Piora had convinced him that he wasn't truly powerless, that he held his own magic. That was enough.

He checked his pocket watch. It was late, but not late enough for her to be asleep yet. He rapped his knuckles against the door, his rings clinking against the wood, and patiently waited to announce to the woman he loved how they would build a future together.

The door slowly opened. His face lit up, only to fall as he realized it was not Piora, but Kaplana who greeted him.

She was in her usual robes, her long hair down in front of her shoulders. She crossed her arms in front of her. "She doesn't want to see you."

Izyk opened his mouth, but she held up her finger. Her whole hand was covered in rings and her wrist had layers of bracelets. Unlike his own jewelry, he doubted hers were fake.

"She let me know she never wants to see you again."

He clenched his teeth. "I don't believe you."

"What you believe doesn't matter because you're not getting past me."

There was an aura of pride radiating from the woman before him. Like she knew he wouldn't attempt to push her aside to get through. And she was right, he wouldn't. But...

"Piora!" he yelled. "Piora, I'm here!"

"Stop that," she hissed quietly. "Before you wake up the whole town."

"Piora!" He refused to yield.

"I can snatch that music hall away from you forever."

Those words shot into him, stopping him immediately. "How do you—"

"I'm the minister, you fool. And, I'm Piora's mother. You don't think I inspected every detail about you, and why exactly you have been spending so much time with my daughter."

He breathed in deeply through his nose, his anger brimming to the surface.

"A shame how the bank plans to destroy it," she crooned, zero sympathy in her words.

"What do you want from me?" What did she want from Piora?

"I want you to leave my daughter alone. She will be competing tomorrow because she still thinks she can win you your stupid music hall, even after I warned her numerous times against it."

"She thinks she can win because her invention is brilliant," he shot back. "She is a master with her powers and has created something worthy of the damned Heart."

"Then you'll both be disappointed with the outcome."

"You'll be disappointed when she finally realizes her worth and never seeks to see you again."

He turned around without another word, but he would have the memory of Kaplana's seething face stamped into his mind forever.

He didn't care what she told him—he didn't believe Piora didn't want to see him. Her mother was hiding something. He only wished he could learn what before tomorrow's fate was decided.

Piora watched Izyk leave from her window. Even with his wool coat on, she saw how his shoulders were deflated. Potek flew by, his feathers a midnight blue. When the bird landed on Izyk's shoulders, Izyk's coat changed to match.

She didn't know why Izyk had visited, but she couldn't handle being around him right now. A void had consumed her, pulling her down into the deepest depths of fear and insecurity.

Without a doubt, Izyk would have reached his hand down to help bring her up, but Piora preferred to wallow alone. Besides, she didn't know how he would handle her self-pity about losing her powers when she had been the one to help him accept his life without ever having any. She would be a hypocrite if she turned around and said her life felt meaningless now.

Maybe he would even agree with her mother, and advise her to not compete so she could become the minister. That thought made her sweater itch against her skin. He would never betray her like that. He trusted her to make her own choice, she reminded herself.

As she looked at the time, she sighed. Tomorrow approached faster than she was ready for it to. She readied herself for bed, but before she laid down, she called upon her lightning powers. Her arms were outstretched, her eyes squeezed shut, her hands trembling at the desperation. Nothing came. Her well was empty, and it would never be refilled.

Her bed squeaked as she fell in between the sheets in hopes she could rest even for a few hours, letting her mind go blank before everything changed tomorrow.

She tossed and turned, and finally she wore herself out enough to let her worries flow away while the Gods entered her dreams.

However, this dream didn't start like the rest. She was on top of the same cliff Izyk had taken her to, her eyes lost in the sea beyond as rain poured down around her, while her clothes and hair stayed dry.

Even if she wanted to turn around or close her eyes, she was stuck in the same position, like her feet were rooted in the dirt below her. She opened her mouth to scream, but no sound came out. It was like she was just another tree amongst the rest of the forest, with nothing special about her anymore. She was nothing, and the Gods were toying with her, laughing at her. A hot tear slid down her cheek, but before she could dwell on her pain much longer, she was shoved over the edge and into the freezing waters below—then yanked out the other side back on land.

She found herself in Ludwik's tavern, once again unable to move, only able to watch. Ludwik was consoling a woman that looked very similar to him. She was crying at the bar, her head in her hands. As Piora leaned forward, she saw bruises dotting the woman's arms.

Then, their words finally reached Piora's ears, but they were muffled, like she was still underwater.

"I'm going to kill him," Ludwik growled.

"He did nothing wrong," the woman next to him, who Piora now guessed had to be his sister, responded while she hiccuped through her tears.

"He hurt you."

"I lost, Ludwik. He's ashamed of me."

"I don't give a fuck that you lost the Undertaking. Your marriage doesn't end because of it."

"He'll be back."

"You have too much faith in him."

"He'll be back," she repeated, but then she leaned away from the bar and touched her abdomen. "He has to."

Ludwik's eyes widened, but Piora didn't see or hear what came next as the dream transitioned.

She was somewhere she had never seen before. A small home, with a crackling fire. At the center of the scene were two people.

"He hasn't shown any signs," a woman with brown, short hair said as she sat on the couch. Her body was practically rolled within itself.

"Maybe he's just a late bloomer," the man next to her offered as a word of comfort, but the woman didn't believe them.

"It's because I lost. The Gods punished me with a worthless, powerless child. Ungifted," she spat.

"Let's not blame anyone."

"He will have nothing to offer this court. He will become destitute."

"He still has time," the man pushed.

"We should leave this court while we're ahead. Perhaps the Rain Court. I could use the warmth and water. We'll leave the boy behind."

"You don't mean that."

"Why not?" The woman turned to him, this time her body was unfurled and alight with excitement. "We can build a new life for ourselves where our past doesn't haunt us."

A loud crash sounded from another room. The two people didn't get up to inspect, but the man called out, "Izyk, come here!"

Piora's heart was in her throat as a boy, no older than five, stepped out. He was dressed in simple nightclothes. She gasped at how similar his face looked to the current Izyk. The only stark difference was that his hair was grown out—the same color as his mother's.

"I don't want you to leave," he whined, and Piora couldn't take it anymore. She wanted to wake up, to get out of this dream, and to curse the Gods for punishing anyone who had lost their Undertaking.

Izyk's father crouched so that he was eye-level with the small boy. Before the man spoke, he turned around to look at Izyk's mother. She nodded sharply.

"We'll only be gone for a while. We'll come back for you."

Piora could see the tears well in Izyk's eyes. She once again attempted to move, to reach out and comfort Izyk, but she was still stuck.

His mother smiled at Izyk, and Piora hated that smile. "You'll figure it out."

Piora sneered at the woman, but her anger couldn't change the past.

Then the scene shifted, and she was lying, strapped to that familiar metal table. She was naked and cold, and swaths of shadows danced around her.

"You disappoint us," a melodic voice whispered in the wind.

"You refuse our call," another one said.

"You will be punished."

"You will be destroyed."

"You will be without a lick of power," a final voice chanted.

The five Weather Gods stormed around her. Their movements were quick, their bodies formless. Then, she felt a stabbing pain near her chest.

She gasped as something was being tugged out of her. A glowing orb of yellow light filtered out, and it was so bright Piora had to squint. It floated up and up, and the shadowy Gods spun around it fast. With each rotation, the light dimmed. Even though this light was outside her body, she felt it inside her, too. One last circle and the light disappeared. Particles of dust fell down on her, and the emptiness from before amplified to an extreme. The Gods brushed along her naked body, a cold chill sweeping across her skin, before they rushed away into the dark. She had no ability to curse the Gods and their cruelty before she was thrown out of the dream.

Nineteen

Piora, along with the rest of the cohort, stood on the other side of the door where their fates would be determined. Outside the workshop, the townspeople bustled around anxiously, waiting to hear if the Lightning Court would survive another year.

Before Piora left, her mother made one last feeble attempt to stop her from competing. Piora shrugged the woman off her, unable to bear her touch. Plus, her mother's begging was fruitless. Piora had lost her Sight. She was officially without an ounce of power.

"You look unwell," Daria approached her. "Like you're going to faint any second."

Piora swallowed. When she woke up from the nightmare, she had vomited. This morning, she couldn't eat, and the effects of being drained of her magic were taking a toll on her.

"Nerves," Piora clarified. The tense energy in the room was palpable. Everyone was keeping to themselves mostly, twiddling their fingers. Piora hated it and couldn't wait for it to end.

"I don't know how the other courts do it."

"What do you mean?"

"Imagine having rocks raining down on you, or having to navigate the violent sea to find the Heart. We just walk in a room."

Piora itched to tell Daria how it wasn't that simple, how walking in that room might doom you to a future so bleak it was difficult to fathom. Instead, Piora kept the truth to herself. She wouldn't fuel the worry—especially when she had strong confidence Daria would be chosen as the worthy inventor.

"The Gods work in mysterious ways" Piora could only offer her friend. Everything that had transpired over the last few months with Izyk, with her mother, with the Gods themselves, had shifted her worldview. No longer would she be blindly devoted to the Gods who ripped families apart. They were cruel, forever enemies in her book.

"Let's hope they work in our favor today."

Piora smiled, but it was half-hearted. She barely had it in her to give more than that.

"Daria, you're first."

The whole room stilled. Daria didn't move an inch, even when Professor Silo called her again.

Piora patted her shoulder. "You got this. Good luck."

Those words shook Daria from her stupor, and finally she slipped past the doors and into the room.

Piora sat on a bench near a window, unable to imagine how whatever happened in the room mattered anymore. When the Gods decided—even if she lost—she had already been punished. What more could they take away from her?

Izyk's future, Piora reminded herself. Thinking about him left an ache in her chest. He would resent her if she lost. He would never want to be with the person who had failed him. He had upheld his end of the deal. She had an invention she was proud of, but she hadn't won him the money.

The room emptied out as others were called. Those who already went waited in a separate room until all competitors had taken their turn. At the end, they would all be called to the main room again, where the ultimate decision would be announced.

"Piora," Professor Silo said.

She looked around and realized she was the last to go.

Getting up, she followed the professor inside. He gestured for her to go to the front of the room.

"I'll be in the other room. All you have to do is show what your invention does. The Heart will flash when it's seen enough. You can knock on that door to bring me back in. Since you're last, the others will join you here."

Piora nodded, acknowledging the words, but they barely sunk in as she looked at the Heart. The topaz gemstone was situated on a stand that rotated. It glowed brightly against the shadows of the dim room. Most would gawk at the wonder of the Heart, but Piora only looked at it with disgust. Memories of it sucking her powers flashed before her, and she could barely stomach standing in it's presence.

Professor Silo exited, and she was alone.

She went up to her invention, which was stationed on a table in front of the Heart. Her finger grazed the button to play Izyk's music but she paused, needing to voice what lay in her heart, hoping for mercy.

"Even if this invention isn't deemed worthy based on whatever made up criteria, please let Izyk find a way to buy the music hall. *He* is worthy of that, and more. He has proven himself dedicated to giving people music that will cause anyone to become transfixed. Listen to his talent."

She pressed the button, and his music poured out of the device. It was like she was swept into a storm, the wind and rain swirling around her, yet she couldn't run from it because of its majesty. She could feel his passion buried within each note. She could feel the way his fingers had trailed against her flushed skin while he drove her mad with desire for his touch and his soul. It was his love in this song, forever stamped into history by the recording.

The music ended, and the room fell into an ominous silence. The Heart flashed rapidly.

She didn't know what it meant that it had allowed her to play the whole song, but she hoped it was enough to convince the Gods of Izyk's worthiness.

She knocked on the door, and the whole cohort filtered back into the room.

Daria reached out her hand, and Piora took it and squeezed. Whatever happened, they would get through it together.

Professor Silo directed up the cohort members into a line. Piora no longer kept her eyes on the Heart. She looked out the window, to the world beyond instead, because that was where what mattered existed. The Gods would never understand what it was like to be here, fighting each day to make it count, to try to remain open and let the beauty in, but failing and getting frustrated, and yet still trying again. The Gods could curse themselves to their meaningless existences, but Piora decided then that whatever was decided, she would live each day appreciating the wonder of it all.

The Heart spun quickly, so fast, Piora thought it would fly off the stand—or worse, it would keep moving, telling everyone in the room no invention was worthy this year, leaving them all doomed. Right when she felt like hope was lost, it stopped suddenly and the light directed itself to Daria.

Izyk had been waiting outside the workshop for what could have been hours. There was a gentle rain coming down on him and everyone else, but no one seemed deterred by it. No one dared complain, for it was whispered that any signs of frustration would lead to their demise; The Undertaking was a reckoning, and no one was above the Gods, so each person here showed their gratitude through prayer and silence. Piora's mother was nowhere to be found, though someone had mentioned she was holding a service at the chapel.

Either way, Izyk's entire focus was on the door that led inside the workshop. He didn't know how Piora was feeling, and it made him want to throw his pocket watch across the street and watch it shatter.

Luckily, his most valuable possession would live to see another day, because just then the workshop's door was practically thrown off its hinges as all the participants came streaming out. There was a storm of chaos as parents, siblings, partners all approached their loved ones. Tears were shed and hugs given in comfort.

Then, there was one woman in the corner with Piora who looked elated, a proud energy brimming. She didn't run to anyone, but the glee across her face revealed exactly who she was.

The winner....which meant it wasn't Piora.

When the two finally separated, Piora caught Izyk's eyes. They were red and blotchy, but Izyk didn't care about anything except going to her and holding her tight. He slowly walked to her, nervous his quick movement would cause her to run. But she stayed still, her arms hugged around herself.

"Hi, Sparkling," he said quietly, so only she could hear.

Her eyes shuttered closed, and she shook her head, as if she couldn't take his presence. He took the moment to assess her. Something was off. It wasn't just losing, there was something else amiss.

And it dawned on him—the consequences of competing and losing. She must have lost her Sight and lightning already. He reached out to pull her in, but even with her eyes shut, she sensed his nearness, because she stepped back.

"I failed you," her voice shook.

"No," he immediately responded, shutting down any of her concerns over him and the music hall. "Are you okay?"

She finally opened her eyes, and they were completely black. No longer did the gold veins streak through them—yet they were never so alluring. He wondered what her skin looked like now. Did that gold vanish, too?

"I didn't uphold my end of the bargain. You must think all the time we spent together was such a waste. I wouldn't blame you for hating me, and never wanting to see me again." She heaved a deep breath as she stopped her rambling.

She must have worn herself out, because she was fluid in his arms as he brought her to his chest and held her tightly. Immediately, she wrapped her arms around his abdomen in response, and for the first time in hours, Izyk could breathe easily. Today would forever be a stubborn stain on Piora's life, he had no doubt, because she held herself to such a high standard. Yet, he knew that if they could survive this together, then they could get through anything the Gods threw their way.

However, Izyk would not let this day be sad and miserable. He had joyful news to share with her, and he wanted to remind her she was more than just a tool to get what he wanted. She was his forever muse, one he held preciously close.

Most importantly, the day wasn't over. He looked at his pocket watch, showing him they had more than enough time to flip the tune of the day into something wondrous and beautiful—and they would do it together.

"Follow me," he said.

Twenty

Celebrations began across the town, and Piora imagined the news had spread throughout the entire court already. Everyone would spend the next few days dancing along the streets, drinking themselves to oblivion, and enjoying the knowledge they would all live another year.

"Hurry," Izyk groaned as he pulled on her arm. They were passing each party, and Piora wanted to join them for a drink so she could forget as much of today as possible. Instead, Izyk led her on as if their lives depended on it.

"What could possibly be more important than the fact the Undertaking was won?"

He suddenly stopped, and Piora crashed into his tall form. He turned around and cupped her cheek. "You are more important, Piora."

Piora swallowed and blushed at the sound of her name from his lips. "I'm not that special. In fact, even the Gods didn't think me worthy." Though knowing what Daria had created, Piora couldn't blame the Gods for choosing the way they did.

Unfortunately for Daria, she would be stuck in meetings and interviews in order to finalize the design of her invention—which she named an ice box—to make it ready for mass production. It would allow food to stay cold longer, and she planned to work with the Snow Court to create a version that would allow the box to get so cold it could freeze things, preserving food for months. Piora had been so proud of her friend, but she could tell Daria wanted to go back to her village and announce the news to her family, to savor their hospitality and pride. It would be weeks before she could get away. Piora promised Daria she would do anything to help relieve any of the stress over the next few weeks so Daria could make it a reality. At some point, she would also need to relay to Daria how she had lost her powers, and how the other cohort members would begin to lose what they most desire, but Piora refused to cloud Daria's special day. She deserved the joy after all she had sacrificed to even compete in the Undertaking.

"They assess your invention—which *I* think is genius—on criteria we don't even know, and the Gods are foolish bastards," Izyk huffed. "It was never about you and your worthiness." He brought her hands up to his lips and pressed a kiss at the center of each palm. "Now, let's go." He tugged on her arm again as he sped onward.

They were in a part of town Piora didn't recognize. The pavement turned to dirt, the woods dark and gray, but she let Izyk drag her. Before long, they were at the mouth of a cave.

Piora cocked her head to the right. "I hope you didn't kidnap me to kill me where no one will hear."

"Not to kill, but I can think of other activities where I make you scream."

"Gross." She shoved him.

"You love it," he shot back.

The words were at the tip of her tongue, the three words she had wanted to voice for days now, but she held them back.

She cleared her throat. "Well...what's so special about this place?"

He smiled down at her, and his bright eyes were like two radiating lights guiding her home.

"It's better if I just let the inside speak for itself."

He took her hand again and brought her inside. At first, it was complete darkness as they entered. A mildewy scent indicated there was water somewhere farther in. As much as she was grateful for the distraction, she didn't really understand why Izyk had brought her here. It was a standard cave. Then, he led her into the next section, and Piora's mouth gaped open.

Little lights flickered throughout the whole room. It was like they were inside a starry night sky.

"What—"

"Fireflies," Izyk replied before she could even finish voicing her question.

"They're beautiful." Piora let go of Izyk to approach the walls to inspect them closely. As she reached the wall, a group of them flew and swarmed her. They floated around her, and for a moment, she forgot how she lost her powers, she forgot about how her mother was a vile being, she forgot about losing. She just had the now in front of her, and it was wonderful and bright. Perhaps, even with the darkness of her new reality, she could learn to find the moments of light. And it was because of the man here with her that she could do that. She turned to him, and he was already staring at her. His eyes matched the bugs around them. Her own personal fireflies. A reminder of the beauty of it all.

"You're beautiful," he finally said, his voice rough and low.

It struck something deep within her heart to see him like this.

"I hope you never doubt how much you mean to me," he added. "How special you are, and how grateful I am that the Gods brought me to you."

"Fuck the Gods," Piora whispered. "They might have brought us together in that chapel, but we nurtured something deeper and more magical than anything they could dare imagine."

Izyk smiled brightly. This time, Piora wasn't scared to say the words.

"I love you, Izyk. So much it hurts to even think of a world where you are not by my side. I know that our deal is done now, even though I failed, but—"

Izyk stepped up to her and placed his hand over her mouth. "Sparkling, I've been waiting to hear those words for ages. I knew you were obsessed with me ever since you kept bumping into me."

She poked at his chest. "You're insufferable."

He bent down so his mouth was next to her ear. "And I'm madly in love with you, too."

It was her turn to smile. She would never get used to being in his presence. He brought her so much joy and peace. She took his chin and guided it down to her lips. They were gentle and slow at first, feeling each breath, each bit of contact, but it wasn't enough. The kiss deepened as he wrapped his arms around her waist and tightened his hold so they were chest to chest.

Breathlessly, she pulled back. "I'm going to help you buy that music hall." She promised it with every bone in her body.

"The music hall doesn't matter as long as I have you."

"You're getting it." And then memories of when her mother tortured her powers out of her came back to her. "I know exactly how, too"

"You look quite mischievous."

"If my mother had no problem taking from me, I don't care about taking from her."

He scrunched his brows at her, but she wiped away his confusion with her thumbs. Piora still had so much to tell Izyk, she realized. He didn't know the whole truth yet. Honestly, she feared he would explode when he learned how her mother had hurt her.

"I'll explain later. Now, I want to take you up on the offer about making me scream so loudly I hope someone mistakes it for an animal ripping me apart."

He didn't say a word, only lifted her sweater off her body and pressed kisses all along her skin. This was why she would continue to keep pushing each day. Even when she had moments where all she felt was the emptiness in her veins, she would have him to fill her up again.

Twenty-One

It was Piora's turn to drag Izyk along through the cobbled streets, wet from the light rain earlier. The celebrations continued, but he could care less about thanking the Gods. Izyk decided then the only person he would go down to his knees for would be the woman in front of him. He would show his gratitude each night as he pressed his lips across her skin, like she was a precious gemstone, holier than the Heart itself.

He loved her so deeply, and finally voicing the words out loud had pushed him off the edge of a cliff where he would keep falling for her everyday.

They took the same path as earlier, which led them right to their beginning destination: the workshop.

"What are we doing here?" he asked as she let go and ran up the few stairs towards the entrance. Without him, he might note. He stepped up to follow, but she turned around before she opened the door and laughed. It was so light and free and beckoning.

"Stop pouting. It'll only take a minute."

He fixed his mouth, barely realizing he was, in fact, pouting. He had become so soft for her, unable to spare a minute of distance. Not after the weeks apart.

As fast as she walked through the doors, she was back out. This time with her recording device in hand.

"Are you going to take me up on my offer to record us as I thrust into you?"

Her face heated to a bright red, as she inspected the area. They were alone though. Everyone else was too preoccupied by drinks and dancing to pay attention to the both of them.

"No," she replied. She amended her statement immediately. "Maybe one day though. After we get your music hall."

He hummed, proud of himself. "It's a deal."

Her face deadpanned at his words, likely reminding her of the time they made their initial bargain.

"Let's go somewhere private."

His earlier cockiness had swept away as concern took over. "What's wrong?"

She lifted the device. "You need to listen."

His heart rate sped up at the vague response, but he took her hand again and brought her to the tavern, where they ignored all the patrons who were too drunk to notice them. As he shut his door, he could sense the worry coming from Piora.

"What's wrong?" he asked again, growing more scared by the second. What had happened to her to cause such a shift?

"You need to control yourself after you listen to this. Do *not* act on any anger. I'm alive, and here, and with you. I survived."

Izyk didn't like the sound of this, and then she pressed the button and he heard Piora's mother, then he heard Piora whining in pain. His hands fisted, and he now understood why Piora prefaced this recording with a warning. His immediate reaction was to run to the chapel where he would beat her mother to a pulp.

Instead, Piora grabbed his arm, reminding him she was there. She guided him towards his bed so he could sit, but nothing could alleviate the anger coursing through him. He could feel the tension across his body, his veins popping up across his forehead and arms.

Piora rubbed his back to soothe him, but it barely worked to calm him. Piora's own mother had stripped Piora of her powers, an act of her own selfishness, and her greed for money. That woman had unforgivably hurt her daughter. He would spend everyday fighting the urge to punish her for it, but he knew the best way to get back at the woman was to remind Piora how she was the most special person to ever exist—powers or not.

As the recording stopped, Izyk shot up from the bed. Perhaps he wouldn't have the strength to hold back his anger.

"Don't, Izyk," she warned. "I didn't have you listen because of what she did to me already. I had you listen so you could hear how we can get back at her."

"Can I be honest?"

She nodded.

"I didn't hear a fucking word that came out of the woman's mouth. I heard your pain and your tears, and the rest didn't matter. I want to end her. I want to hear her scream for mercy as I rip each limb from her body for hurting you."

"I know, but you can't."

"Why?"

"Because she's our key to the music hall."

"How?"

Piora snorted. "If you were listening, you would have heard she said I could have her money if I didn't compete."

"And?" He didn't care if he was being short-tempered and difficult.

"And...we can play a small part of the recording as proof to the banker that I can access her account."

His shoulders slumped down as the reality hit him. In order to come up with this idea, she had to think back about this horrid torture, or perhaps the memory of it was stuck like a second skin, leaving her unable to not think about it. Either way, he would work like hell to erase it from her mind.

"We should use the recording to get her thrown into prison," he seethed.

"If we did that, then she would lose all her money, and we would have nothing."

"I don't care about the music hall if she's still walking around freely."

"I want this. Let me do this for you. Let's take the money back and give it where it's needed. Let's revive this court so art and magic can come together again."

Her eyes were wide and raw with emotion. He could fall to his knees right then and there for how caring she was even after facing such pain and horror.

"Will that recording be enough to convince the banker?"

Piora shrugged. "It will be unprecedented for the bank, but it's her voice. We might as well try."

"Are you sure?" He needed to hear her say it, to acknowledge she was okay with using this to help him.

She cupped his cheek. "There is nothing I wouldn't do to see you shine."

Piora had her hands in between her legs, hiding the shakiness that had taken over as soon as they entered the bank. She didn't know what to expect. This idea was risky, but she would do it for the man beside her.

Clearly, she wasn't hiding her anxiety well, because Izyk pulled her hand out and placed it in his lap. He drew small lines in her palm, soothing her just enough to breathe deeply again.

"Whatever happens, we walk out of here together," he said, consoling her. She knew he would never resent her for not winning him the money, but...after everything, she wanted it, too. She wanted something to work on with her hands, to help bring the abandoned building to new life again, along with those dead streets so that those that were labeled ungifted could be welcomed back to a thriving town. She wanted to find a purpose now that her veins no longer pumped with the essence of lightning, and she was no longer burdened by the Weather Gods haunting her dreams.

"Together," she promised him.

Right as Izyk leaned over to press a kiss to her cheek, Blysk groaned as he sat down.

"I heard you finally have the funds, Izyk," the banker said, skeptical. He tapped on the shiny, clean desk in front of him, waiting.

"I have it," Piora amended.

Blysk shifted his attention to her, almost surprised by her presence next to Izyk, "And you are?"

"Piora, minister Kaplana's daughter."

The banker's countenance changed at that. "That account is kept locked up, only for your mother to access."

"She gave me permission."

"I would need to hear it from her or—"

"I have her word."

"That is not enough. I need to hear it myself."

She practically slammed the recording device on the desk, but slowed down at the last minute as to not break it. She pressed the button, and her mother's words floated free.

"…You are allowed to access my bank account and to do whatever you want with the money—"

Piora stopped the device.

"See?" She gestured to the air. "I have my mother's word, and now you've heard it."

"I—" he stammered, unsure how to move forward, no doubt.

Piora and Izyk knew it was a long shot, and the way the banker hesitated didn't increase her confidence. She had to push further.

"I don't think going against the minister's words will do you any favors. She has access to the Gods, and she would gladly relay how you refuse to listen to her."

The banker swallowed, while Izyk squeezed Piora's hand. She quickly glanced at Izyk, and he seemed to be staring at the wall behind the banker's desk, refusing to make eye contact with anyone. He was nervous. She would do anything to alleviate his worry. She would go to her knees in front of the banker and beg him to let her get the money out.

She turned back at the banker, who still seemed to be thinking. This was it. Everything would be determined by this moment. What Izyk and her future would look like came down to this one man standing in the way of it all.

"Right this way," he finally said.

Epilogue

The rain drenched her, but the booms of thunder and flashes of lightning revitalized her. Even with her eyes closed, she could still see the effects of the storm behind her lids, the way it swayed the trees nearby, coated the streets with puddles, and caused an abrupt chaos to her life. She could even picture Potek flying the skies with his constantly-changing colored feathers.

She reached out a hand, calling the weather down to her, to touch it again, and to let it flow back to her. But it remained only around her. Never again would she be one in the same with the cloudy skies.

Her tears mixed with the rain, but she refused to be sad. Sacrifices were made, a part of her forever lost in the mist and wind. It didn't ache anymore, though—the emptiness. She filled it with new things. She joined Izyk everyday to fix up the music hall. She worked with Daria to develop her invention further with delegates from the Snow Court. She moved away from her mother—her mother, who had been livid when she had learned the majority of the money she had been saving for herself had been used. Piora didn't care, just like she would never care what the Gods had to say about the lying she had to do to get it.

Now, she and Izyk found an old home, not too far from the music hall. It would also need fixing at some point, along with the other buildings surrounding it, but they would worry about that after today. After the inaugural performance, where hundreds of people, both gifted and ungifted, would be watching.

"There you are," Izyk practically screamed over the loud pitter-patter of the downpour. "I love that you are still so in tune with your roots, Sparkling, but I cannot perform looking like a wet dog."

She smiled. "I think the people would love it. Your shirt would be all wet. They could see your beautiful form that you're always hiding under your coat."

He rubbed his chin, thinking about it. "Perhaps I would sell more tickets that way. Maybe we take it a step farther, and I go shirtless."

"Now, you're pushing it." She turned to him finally.

"Would you get jealous?"

"No," she said too quickly to mean it.

"What are you thinking?" he asked, his tone changing.

"I'm thinking I'm scared." He stayed quiet, allowing her to voice what she needed. "What if this fails? Will I grow to resent everything I did to get here? Then, I feel guilty for allowing my thoughts to go there, because I could never regret whatever path led me to you."

"I think," he started, stepping up to her and taking her chin in his hands so she was staring right into those golden brown eyes. "It's okay you feel that way. I have days where I fear this will all be for nothing, but I remember it could not have been, because you're next to me. My dream started with buying this music hall, but it ended with having you in my arms for the rest of my life."

She wiped at her eyes as she took in his love.

"And I'm also thinking...my words will never be enough to convey what you mean to me, and I'm hoping the song you inspired will."

When Izyk had mentioned he finally composed something that would be the perfect piece for opening night, she desperately wanted to hear it right then and there, but he refused. He told her she deserved hearing it only when they had a full orchestra, when she sat in a plush velvet chair with all the lights dim except for the spotlight on stage. She couldn't wait to finally hear their story poured from his master mind.

Potek chirped from where he soared above, as if he was congratulating Izyk for what he had accomplished. They had been watching each other for years, and now they could thrive together.

Izyk wrapped his arms around her shoulder and pulled her towards the music hall, where they would need to dry up and get ready for the night that would be the beginning of their future.

There had always been something missing in her life, a void that even winning the Undertaking wouldn't have filled. Her powers hadn't been enough, either. After losing it all, and learning to accept whatever lay ahead, Piora realized Izyk was that missing piece; as was her freedom to choose him to fulfill it.

Acknowledgements

Another one down and another set of thank you's to write!

Des, my wonderful, spectacular, amazing—insert all the adjectives here—editor. Thank you for taking care of my words and for bringing these stories to new heights.

Aubrey, once again, I am stunned with how you're able to take my ideas and make them better than I could have imagined. I always get so excited when I get to see your work, and your covers truly have made this series extra special.

Lemmy, you beautiful and hardworking soul. Thank you for working endlessly to find a dedicated group of ARC readers. You have created and fostered such a lovely community, and I hope you're proud of what you've done in such a short time already.

I've said it a few times, but this story was the easiest one to write for some reason. The words flowed, and there was magic in the air as Piora and Izyk came alive on page for me.

Readers, I hope you loved them as much as I do. You deserve the last and biggest THANK YOU! Thank you for reading my stories. Your positive words are the light that keep me writing each day, through all the doubts and fears about this author venture I decided to embark on. I will never be able to thank you all enough!

About the Author

KC Silver is a born and raised Chicagoan, spending her days exploring the city, one train stop at a time. She currently works as a media planner at a large media agency where she daydreams of the day when a Slack notification no longer makes her heart jump in fear.

KC enjoys character driven stories where the main character is on a journey of discovering themselves and learning to let go of the expectations weighing on them, while falling in love.

She can be found on all socials @bysilverstories